THE LITTLE PINK PILL

By

K. L. Smith

For my late-husband Shaun – who was my life

Chapter One

My routine in the morning is always the same. Get up, get washed, get dressed and take my tablet. I never used to like routine in my life before the head injury; in fact, I think it's fair to say that I avoided routine at all costs. Now though, I can't function without it.

I think it's something to do with the way that my brain is rewired now, it isn't very good at making on the spot decisions but it runs sufficiently well on autopilot. It does lately anyway.

Once I've had my risperidone - which my wife Linda calls my little pink pill, my head gets foggy for a while and it's difficult to really *feel* things in the way that I used to, emotionally. I can remember what it was like to feel, I just don't have those emotions anymore.

Normally once the tablet takes effect, I join my wife at the garden centre that she set up a few years ago. I can't deal with the public or anything like that, but I can do odd jobs around the place to help out. At least it gives me something useful to do.

Today however, is a break from my routine, today I have to visit my new psychologist Dr Patel.

It was a big deal that I was trusted to attend the appointment on my own; it would have been unthinkable at one time. I couldn't go anywhere without Linda hanging onto me for dear life, just in case I should try and attack someone. She's been through a lot looking after me and I don't think I would still be alive if not for her.

I think if I *could* feel I would love her.

I arrived at the hospital five minutes early, I don't like being late and I don't tolerate bad punctuality in others. I was shown through to the waiting room with four minutes to spare - three minutes once I'd been weighed. I have never understood why I have to be weighed. I dislike things that are unnecessary.

My appointment was supposed to start at eleven o'clock sharp, but by eleven-fifty-five I was still waiting. Before I used to have the little pink pill I could not stand to be in a situation like this. Locked in a waiting room full of noisy people all talking at once, hysterical children screaming their lungs out, irate Mothers screaming back at them. No sense of urgency in the staff at all in the way they were sluggishly shepherding patients through.

In the old days I would have exploded by now, possibly hit a few people before a doctor would come running to sedate me. Now though, I can sit here calmly annoyed watching the clock on the wall, waiting for the doctor to call me in to waste my time.

Finally, I was shown through to the cramped little office at the end of the hall. I shuddered at the cold clinical room, only a small window high up on the wall attempted to illuminate the dismal space.

"Ah now, Mr Locke." The young Asian doctor beckoned me to take a seat before offering me his hand. I was relieved that he offered his right hand; I didn't like the look of disgust on people's face if they were forced to shake my mutilated left hand.

"Hello Doctor." I nodded in greeting.

"Very good to meet you Mr Locke, as you know Dr Mandela sadly passed away a little while ago, and so I will be doing my best to take over in her place."

He made good eye contact with me without staring too hard, so that seemed okay.

When I didn't respond, he carried on. "Do you mind if I ask you a few questions?"

I shook my head. I really didn't care.

"May I call you Flynn?"

"Yes."

"Good. Well Flynn, I see from your notes that you have suffered a severe brain trauma a number of years ago. What caused the head injury, if I may ask?" He sat back in his chair looking expectantly at me.

I sighed, I didn't like going over it all the time, I felt like a stuck record playing out a scene that I didn't really remember very well. The words came out pre-rehearsed and false sounding even to my own ears.

"I was on a bus when a suicide bomber detonated a bomb."

He wheeled his chair forwards a little with curiosity. "You don't mean you were on *that* bus?"

"Yes. My wife and I. She was facing the window at the front; we were just about to get off when it happened. She was knocked unconscious instantly and didn't wake up until she was in an ambulance. Luckily for her she never saw any of it coming and only suffered concussion." I fiddled subconsciously with my mangled finger stumps.

"And what about you Flynn? What happened to you? What do you remember about it?"

"I banged my head hard." I held my hand up to my forehead. "I suffered damage to my left frontal lobe, and my fingers blew off. I remember what I saw but I don't want to talk about it."

He looked at me for a while folding his hands into steeples. "Okay Flynn, I understand that you don't want to revisit something so traumatic, but have you ever been for counselling? It can be very helpful."

I nodded. "I went twice but was barred after I bit the councillor."

Dr Patel looked like he almost laughed then, but managed to reign it back in before he looked too unprofessional. "Why did you bite the councillor?"

"She was too loud and she got too in my face. I don't like loud noises it makes me angry. It *did* make me angry." I corrected myself. "Now with the pink pill I can control it better."

"Pink pill?" He looked down at his notes. "Risperidone?"

"Yes."

"How long have you been taking it for?"

"A couple of years."

"That's a major drug for you to be taking. Are you aware that it is an anti-psychotic normally used to treat schizophrenia?"

"Yes. Dr Mandela said it would help and she was right, it did. She said my behaviour due to the left frontal lobe damage was very much like schizophrenia."

"In what way?"

I didn't like all these questions but I knew the faster I answered them the faster I could go home.

"I couldn't control my behaviour. I had blackouts where I would act out, hurt people, and then snap out of it not remembering what I'd done."

"That could be a form of epilepsy Flynn."

I shook my head. "I've been tested, I'm not epileptic. As long as I take the pink pill I'm fine."

He looked thoughtfully at me. "How do you feel now?"

"I don't feel anything."

"In what sense?"

"I don't feel happiness or sadness, anger, any emotion really." I shrugged. "I'm sort of numb."

"Is this since the risperidone?"

"Yes."

"Okay." He looked around him for a moment. "Do you have a partner?"

"Yes, my wife Linda."

"Is Linda the one who was on the bus with you?"

"Yes." I already said that. I thought he was supposed to be intelligent?

"Is she supportive of you? Does she help you cope?"

"She's looked after me from the start. She wasn't traumatised like I was; she didn't see what I saw. Although before the pink pill I thought she was the crazy one. I was convinced that she was a psycho that was trying to kill me."

He looked sympathetic. "I understand how different the world can look after a serious head trauma; perception can be a tricky thing to navigate when you're brain-damaged."

He looked at the clock on the wall. "I'm afraid that will have to be all for today, but I'd like to see you again next week if that's alright with you? I'm sure that there is more we can do to help."

Inwardly I was annoyed, but outwardly I agreed.

Chapter Two

My hospital appointment had left me tired and agitated, plus because of my appointment being late, I had got caught up in the lunchtime traffic. I sat at the traffic lights in frustration at the stupid old woman in front of me that kept stalling every time she tried to set off. I took a deep breath and counted to ten. In my head I started to tune in and listen to the song that's always hiding away in there, somewhere towards the back. *'Never tear us apart'*, by *INXS*. I don't particularly like it but it does distract me from things when I get irate.

I felt my pulse slow and my shoulders relax. The old woman ahead finally got her car to move and I set back off. I decided to go straight home to lie down for a while, I wasn't up to working today, I was too exhausted.

Many hours later my wife was home.

"Hello darling." She addressed me as she came in. She looked pretty today. She's always been attractive but today she looked especially nice, not looking her age of forty, one bit. Unlike me - that was already going a little grey around the temples. We were the same age but she was definitely weathering better than me.

"How did you get on with the new doctor?" I could tell she was concerned but was doing a good job of trying to hide it.

"He was okay. Nice enough. The trouble is he wants me to go back again next week."

She looked puzzled. "What for? Dr Mandela only ever wanted to see you once every three months."

"I don't know. New doctor syndrome? Thinks he knows more than any of the other doctors I've seen before."

She walked over to the fridge and pulled a bottle of milk out. "Well I'll come with you next time. We can't have him messing with your medication like the others have."

I put the kettle on while she busied herself with the cups. I decided to try a little small talk, as she seemed to like that. "How did it go at work today?"

She smiled. "It was really good actually, business is definitely picking up. Takings have gone up a lot this week."

"That's really good." I faked a smile at her, but she looked away. I think I need more practice with my expressions; I'd practice tonight in the bathroom mirror after I brushed my teeth.

In my old life I used to be fun. I went out of my way to woo my wife while we were both still in university. She hated me at first sight, but I loved her. I did the usual things that a boy in love does. When she ignored me, I let her bicycle tyres down. When she noticed me but thought I was an idiot, I perpetuated that thought by acting like an idiot. I followed her, stalked her, sang to her, sent chocolates to her…

When she kicked me for being creepy I upped my game by following a piece of worldly advice my friend gave me. I told her that I didn't like her anymore; I didn't know what I could've been thinking. Now I'd come to my senses I realised I much preferred her best friend Liz. I then turned all my attention on the said best friend Liz. To my amazement, my little ploy worked. Linda - who had got used to me chasing her constantly, suddenly found herself annoyed that my attention was now for Liz only. She suddenly found she quite liked my idiotic ways after all; she even went so far as to say I was 'quirky'.

Before long we were living together. Next came marriage, then mortgage, and then miscarriage. Our full life together suddenly seemed not quite so fun after all. But, we had each other through thick and thin. After many more miscarriages we gave up on the idea of children. It hurt too much to keep trying and to keep losing, there's only so much anyone can take.

We threw ourselves into our respective careers, me as a photographer, Linda as a botanist. For a while life was trundling along well, until the London trip anyway.

I shook my head; it was pointless thinking about the past. It was gone. Here was the now, and now, I was tired. I got into bed and turned my brain off for the day.

I opened my eyes to the dream again. I was back on the number 30 bus. Looking around me I could see that I was on the top deck this time. My nose filled with the acrid smell of diesel fumes and cigarette smoke, it made my nostrils sting a little. Someone should remind me when I'm awake that smoking has been prohibited on buses for years.

I don't like the light here, it seems very unnatural, an almost suffocating repulsive orange, it sets my teeth on edge and makes my skin hurt. If I was capable of feeling anything I probably would be nervous.

The very air on this bus seemed to radiate an electric current. Looking around me I could see I was the only passenger tonight. I got off the bench seat and made my way down the steps to the bottom deck and apprehensively made my way towards the front. If I could ring the bell hopefully this awful bus would stop and I could get off. I saw a button bell installed on one of the metal supports behind the driver's cabin. I made my way shakily over to it and pressed it for all I was worth but alas no sound.

In desperation I decided to ask the driver to stop. I moved a few steps further down until I was level with him. "Can I please get off?"

As he turned to face me I could see that it was *me* that was driving. "Hey Flynn." 'The other me' grinned from under his driver's cap. "Where to tonight?"

"Let me off."

"Aw don't be like that Flynn you only just got here. Plus, you already bought a ticket."

"I didn't." As a pointed at him I realised I had a bus ticket it my hand. I tried to flick it off with fright. It was stuck to my skin of my miraculously reattached fingers as if with superglue. "Get if off." I panicked, as it starting to burn. As I flapped at it I saw the destination and return address on the ticket.

FROM: - Marble Arch

TO: - Daynejonne

"Please get it off!" I yelled as my fingers started to melt and drip to the floor. I screamed at the top of my lungs. "PLEASE HELP!!"

I opened my eyes to blackness with my heart racing.

"Flynn it's okay. It's just a bad dream. Everything's fine." Linda flicked the light on and held me until I could stop shaking. I looked at her, prostrate with fear.

"Everything is fine," she said soothingly. "You're safe with me. I promise nothing will hurt you."

I nodded my understanding and lay in her arms for an hour or more. Once I calmed down she asked, "What did you dream?"

"I don't dream." I lied.

Got up, washed and dressed. Took the little pink pill. Went numb, went to work. This was a good day.

Routine is good now, knowing exactly what is going to happen, when it's going to happen, and how it will happen. I dislike the unknown.

Linda is a real people person; she can talk for hours with her customers about everything under the sun, whereas I avoid people like the plague.

My day was going well until a young woman approached me holding a tray of pansies while I was just putting up a hanging basket onto a hook.

"Excuse me!" She shouted at me. "Hey you! Yes you!" She chased after me as I walked away. "Do you work here?"

I was annoyed but held my pink-pilled temper, fortunately for her.

"I only help out." I told her. "If you need to speak to someone speak to Linda on the till." I started to turn away from her as she grabbed my arm.

"Hey don't walk away from me! I want to make a complaint."

I looked down at her fingers tightly wrapped around my arm and felt the heat rise up through my chest. My fists started to clench and my teeth were getting ready to bite.

"Whoa there." Linda came running up and prised the bitch's fingers off my arm. She turned to me. "Be a love Flynn and go put the kettle on quick." She smiled nervously at me.

I eyeballed my potential victim and trotted off to the back room to do as I had been bid.

Once I was sat in the back room drinking a cup of coffee I was fine again. After several more cups of coffee, I was much more relaxed. I think I even nodded off for a while.

I shook myself awake properly and was surprised to see no sign of Linda. I ventured out and had a look around for her. Nope. No sign. I noticed she'd put the closed sign on the main door. Where was she? Had I fallen asleep?

I was just getting ready to go home when she came around the corner and made me jump.

"Good god you scared me!" She claimed holding her chest in shock.

"You made me jump." I retorted. "Where were you?"

"After that horrid woman went I decided to close for the day. I've been stacking all of the dead tomato plants onto the compost heap, then I got watered up everywhere. I came by a little while ago but you were fast asleep."

"Was I? I wasn't sure if I had been to sleep."

"It'll be the stress of that woman getting too close and up in your face. It's not that long ago you would have punched her for doing that."

I nodded. "Without a doubt."

She took my arm in hers. "Come on let's go home."

I couldn't sleep that night. I kept revisiting the scene in my head from earlier. For a brief moment, I had felt something. When that woman wrapped her fingers around my arm and shouted at me, I felt the start of something, something intoxicating. After two years of feeling nothing to suddenly really feeling something, it felt like heroin.

And I think I wanted more.

I lay awake all night wondering what would happen if I stopped taking the pink pill. Could I fool people into thinking I was still taking it? I had worn the mask of numbness for two years, could I 'emperor's new clothes' it and pretend the mask is still on?

In all honesty I couldn't feel enough to care.

My experiment would begin tomorrow.

Got up, got washed, got dressed, spat pink pill down the toilet. I smiled a real smile at the new addition to my routine. I faked numbness and went to work.

I stayed at work for the first hour or so but disappointment soon chased me out of there. There was nothing here today to make my heart race. I told Linda I had a headache and that I was going home to lie down. She kissed me on the lips and told me she loved me. That stirred something in me, but it wasn't love, it was definitely lust. But, I had to pretend to be numb. I looked away before she could see the look that I couldn't get out of my eyes.

I left with a backwards wave.

Fuck going home to lie down. I was going OUT!

I had forgotten just how exhilarating driving can be. Normally I drove slowly and carefully, mindful that the slightest little thing I did wrong might result in my licence being revoked by the medical board. But not today. Today I laughed like only a mad man can as I wove in and out of the midday traffic. I blasted my horn at dawdling pedestrians; tail gaited, gave everyone the finger, and generally made myself as much of a nuisance as I could. I hadn't felt that alive in years. I could feel my heart thudding against my ribcage with the adrenalin rush I was giving it. I felt invincible, a predator, fast, powerful, sleek and dangerous.

The world was mine.

Although I had forgotten how powerful my mood swings could be without the pink pill.

After I parked up in the city centre I had a change of heart and a mild panic attack at the thought of all of the people I had just upset.

What had I been thinking not taking the pink pill? I thumped the steering wheel with temper. I had just started to rebuild my life again, becoming a member of society again. I could lose my wife, my job, my home, god my *freedom* if Linda decided to have me committed.

What the hell was wrong with me? I rested my head against the steering wheel, fighting back the fear in my heart. Within the blink of an eye I had gone from being powerful to a coward. I lifted my head back up and started to smile again. I was feeling panic! That was an old acquaintance I hadn't seen for a while. He and I used to be bosom buddies in the old days.

I sat there for almost an hour absorbing all the emotions that had hit me like a tidal wave. Fear, anger, fury, eventually descending into sadness and guilt. It was too much too soon. I'd had enough for one day and headed home to take the pink pill.

Chapter Three

For the next few days I behaved myself. There wasn't really anything wrong with being numb. I had routine; I knew what was going to happen, when it would happen and how it would happen. After the head injury my life had been chaos and I couldn't go back to that. It wasn't fair on Linda. With what I was like in the first few years following the head injury, anyone else would have had me committed, but she stood by me and looked after me. She cleaned the house back up after I trashed the place, bandaged my wrists back up every time I slit them, spent countless hours with her fingers down my throat making me vomit up the pills I had overdosed with.

To my shame - or at least when I could feel shame, I think I may also have hurt Linda a few times. I had a lot of blackouts where I would do things that I have no memory of. Many times after these blackouts I would wake up on the floor to find Linda covered in blood, or bruised and battered. She used to comfort me and tell me she knew it wasn't really me that had done it. She knew it was 'the other' me. I would cry for days at the hurt I couldn't remember but must have inflicted on her. This usually led me to trying to kill myself again.

It's terrible waking up out of a blackout. It must be what it would be like to be possessed by a demon if such things existed. It's like a total stranger had been running riot in my body for a few hours, doing whatever the hell he pleases and then when he's had his fun he departs leaving me to pick up the pieces. I shudder to think of the things 'other me' must have done.

I once woke up in the car covered in blood that wasn't mine, but I'm not supposed to talk about that.

Today was my second appointment with Dr Patel. Linda had managed to get someone to cover for her at work so that she could come with me.

Once again I was sitting in the annoying waiting room full of noisy people all talking at once. The hustle and bustle of dozens of people all crammed into a confined space was very overwhelming. But, I was tolerating all of this very well I thought. Linda however was not. She kept looking at the clock on the wall that showed we had been waiting forty minutes past our appointment time. She was tapping her feet impatiently and clenching her jaw.

"They know very well that you don't cope with noise. Why the hell can't they give you an appointment that they can actually keep?"

"I'm okay." I replied to reassure her.

"It's *not* okay. It's the same every time. Why tell you to come at twelve o'clock if they won't see you till one o'clock? Why lock you in a room full of noisy people when one of the reasons you are here is that you can't cope with noisy people!" Her voice was getting louder and people were starting to look.

I repeated. "I'm okay."

She sat back in her seat looking annoyed.

One thing I had noticed since the head injury and from other brain-damaged people who shared this thought with me; our carers get so used to adapting our surroundings for us so that we don't get agitated, that when the environment around us becomes out of their control, they get more agitated then we do. They react to things before we have a chance to.

At home she always made sure to control the volume on the TV. She always muted the noisy adverts before they had chance to annoy me. She replaced all of the light bulbs in the house with low wattage ones that wouldn't hurt my eyes and give me a headache. She wouldn't let anyone in the house who wouldn't regulate their voice to a softer tone. I have also noticed she gets anxious if noisy people are anywhere near me. If I get seated in a café too near to the door, as I dislike people being behind me, she insists on us being moved or she'll take me straight out of there. She reacts so that I won't.

I should feel bad that her life has had to adapt around me so much.

Finally, we were called in.

"Mr and Mrs Locke please come in and take a seat."

We followed Dr Patel into his office and sat down. "Good to see you again Flynn, and very nice to meet you Mrs Locke." He shook both of our hands.

"Please call me Linda."

"Very good, thank you Linda." He smiled at her. "So how are you Flynn?" He asked turning towards me.

"I'm fine."

Dr Patel looked over at Linda with mild amusement.

"He's doing alright." She smiled over at me nervously. "No mood swings, no blackouts, very even tempered."

Dr Patel looked down at his notes. "Last time we spoke Flynn, you mentioned a lack of emotion since you've been on the risperidone?"

"That's right." I wondered briefly if I should mention the morning I had spat the pill out, then thought better of it. Best to keep that to myself.

"Do you mind if I ask Linda a few questions Flynn? I don't wish to sound rude it will just give me a clearer picture of how you're coping. Is that okay with you?"

"That's fine." I didn't mind, I would rather not have to speak anyway. I sat back and let them get on with it. I was more interested in the small spider I could see crawling down the skirting board.

"Linda, Flynn mentioned last time about suffering from blackouts before he was prescribed Risperidone. Could you describe the blackouts for me?"

She looked uncomfortable. "Well, they normally occurred after something stressful had happened."

"Such as?"

"Well, for example, a couple of years ago a woman in a shop was rude to him and he reacted badly and ended up screaming at the top of his lungs at her. I mean REALLY screaming. I dragged him home with the help of my neighbour. Once he was home he went really quiet and started trembling with rage. His face went purple and then he seemed to sort of fall into a trance. He stared for a minute or two at me, and then leaped up with superhuman strength and threw me against a wall. He was like a demon." She looked over at me apologetically. "It was like his body had been taken over by someone else, he didn't even look like the same person. I know it must sound strange to you, but you have to see it to believe it." She reached over and held my hand. I know she felt bad about bad mouthing me.

Dr Patel looked like he was thinking about what she had said. "You say he was like someone else?"

"Yes." She looked over to me for confirmation. "We call him 'the other one'.

"The other one?"

She looked at her feet. "Flynn is the most gentle kind person I have ever met. He would never in a million years hurt a hair on my head. He would defend me with his dying breath from anyone." She paused. "But when he had a blackout he became the opposite of everything that he is. He turned into a sadist. Then after he'd frightened the shit out of me, my lovely gentle husband would return who had no clue what had happened to me. He'd be devastated at the sight of the blood and bruises thinking that we must've been attacked by someone. The only way I can keep my sanity and not take it out on Flynn is to separate him from the other one. Flynn is Flynn, the other one, is the other one."

Dr Patel was hanging off her every word. He was practically falling off his seat. I wondered if he was hankering after doing a study on me. Maybe he had an eye on a Nobel Prize?

"This is most fascinating. I see from Flynn's notes that his tests for epilepsy came back negative. These blackouts as you call them do sound remarkably like schizophrenia or rather dissociative-identity-disorder, sometimes known as multiple-personality-disorder. Tell me, did anything like this ever happen before the head injury?"

We both shook our heads.

"Interesting. Would you object to another brain scan Flynn?" He asked turning to me.

"I don't mind."

"Good, good." He wrote something down and then turned back to me. "I see from your notes that you only stayed in hospital for two days after the brain injury. That seems a little strange."

Linda nodded. "We were told that because he didn't have a bleed on the brain and there was no un-due pressure in his skull that he wouldn't have to stay in for very long other than to come back to the out-patients clinic once a month. Pretty much as soon as he could tell the doctors what day it was and name the current Prime Minister he was sent home."

Dr Patel shook his head. "That is shocking. He should at least have gone for rehabilitation care before being sent home."

"He should. It was a lot to cope with on my own."

He shook his head in sympathy at her before turning to me and returning to his questions. "Can you tell me anything else about your behaviour after the head injury?"

I was getting sick of all the questions so I looked to Linda. "Linda can tell you better then I can."

He turned to her. "What can you tell me Linda?"

"Goodness where to start." She looked up thoughtfully before continuing. "The mood swings were the first things that I noticed. He could go from being insanely happy one moment, to suddenly being in floods of tears the next. After a while I noticed a pattern starting. He would find the most ridiculous things hysterical, he would get like a giddy child, but the dramatic high would be followed by a dramatic low. He would suddenly crash into the depths of despair, normally ending in a suicide attempt." She paused. "Also he became very inappropriate."

"In what way inappropriate?"

"Well you know how everyone has an inner monologue?"

"Yes."

"He would say anything and everything that came into his head, regardless of how hurtful it was. He'd tell the whole world about his sex life, bowel movements, masturbating techniques etc."

I nodded my agreement.

"Anything else?" Dr Patel asked her.

"He became delusional. He went through a stage of thinking I was trying to kill him. He called me a psycho and a monster for a while. He tried to sleep with a carving knife under his pillow for a while for 'protection' he said." She shook her head at her own words.

"Do you remember any of this Flynn?" Dr Patel asked me with interest.

"Some of it. The way she describes 'the other one' is how I saw her for a while. I really thought for a while that she might kill me. I know that it's ridiculous now, if she wanted me dead why would she keep saving my life every time I tried to kill myself? I thought she was having affairs with all of the neighbours. I once thought she had deliberately moved all of the furniture around in the living room just to mess with my head. I don't know, to me I was the normal one, it was the rest of the world that had suddenly gone mad."

"And this all stopped when you started taking the risperidone?"

"Yes."

"Thank you both for coming in today, it's been very informative. This might be an imposition, but would you mind coming in once a week to see me for a little while Flynn? If it's convenient of course. This is an intriguing case and I'd like to do a little more research. There might be a better pill than risperidone that will control the mood swings but not make you feel quite so, numb, I believe you called it?"

We both agreed outwardly, while inwardly cringing.

Chapter Four

It's been three days since I saw Dr Patel and I have been good. Every day I've stuck to my routine. Got up, got dressed, took the pink pill, went numb, went to work. Today I'm doing an experiment again.

Linda kept eyeballing me all day; I don't think I was acting any different to 'normal' but she certainly kept watching me. I almost gave the game away when a young boy fell over a fern and I started laughing before I could help myself. My god if felt good to laugh. I had to go outside while I composed myself and fixed my face back into its 'normal' blank slate.

An hour later I nearly slipped again when a pretty young woman smiled at me. Before I could stop myself I beamed back at her. She stayed talking to me for around eight minutes before Linda appeared looking suspicious. If I was going to keep this up I'd have to learn to hide it better.

To my delight later on, I found that the young lady had slipped her phone number into my pocket. My heart was racing with the adrenalin. Did everyone else feel this alive all the time?

By two o'clock I made my excuses to Linda to leave. I couldn't keep up the blank face, a smile kept appearing involuntarily on my lips. I was going to get found out and sentenced to numbness again.

I didn't go straight home as I told Linda I would, instead I went to the park and sat on the swings for a while. Thankfully I was the only person there, I hadn't liked the thought of being mistaken for a paedophile, but the urge to swing on a swing had been over powering ever since I saw a child on a swing on a TV advert earlier.

Looking around me to make sure I was alone, I pulled the swing back with my feet and let rip. I screamed with delight as I flew up and down through the air. It was magical. I laughed and laughed and laughed.

How could children be stuck indoors on their games consoles when they could be playing on swings? This was wonderful. I skidded the swing to a stop as my heart suddenly sank. Oh no. How the hell could I go home and look numb? I was too happy! This had been wonderful, but it would show on my face wouldn't it?

My giddiness started to drop, my heart rate increased and I went cold. God, Linda would know! As soon as she saw me she would know! I put my head in my hands. How could I do this to her? Oh god! I hit the side of my head with frustration. I could feel my pins starting to prick at my eyes, please no don't let me cry. But I did.

After that I felt a little better.

I went home and arrived just before Linda did, just before she could see me taking a half of the little pink pill.

I don't know how long I'd been asleep when I opened my eyes to find myself back on the number 30 bus. It seemed to be night-time on the bus, so where this awful orange glow came from was beyond me. Once again the smell of diesel fumes mixed with stale cigarette smoke filled my nostrils making me feel sick. Tonight there was music playing on the bus, 'Never tear us apart' by INXS. I hate that song.

"Shame you don't like it. I'm only playing it for you." The 'other one' said from across the bus.

"Why do I keep hearing this bloody song? It's always in my head." I grumbled.

"Why do you think? Any way I just wanted to meet up with you to tell you how much I like the experiment that you're doing." He got up and walked over to me, sitting on the bench in front of me but turning around to face me.

"How do you know about the experiment?"

"Who do you think came up with the idea?" He grinned.

I didn't like the way he smiled at me. He reminded me of a shark. Was that what my smile looked like to Linda? I wondered.

"I just wanted to *feel* for a little while." I sulked.

"And so you should. Do you still have the phone number that woman gave you?"

"Yes."

"Use it." He licked his lips.

"No. I love Linda."

"Why? She tried to kill you."

"She didn't."

"Well she tried to kill me." He countered.

"I'll kill you." I went to grab his throat but my fingers fell off before I could get a good hold.

"AGGHHH!" I screamed down at the bloody stump that was all that was left of my left hand.

He'd vanished.

"Looking for these?" He called from behind me.

I turned at the sound of his voice as he threw my bloody fingers back at me.

I woke up in a panic in the dark again.

The following day, I got up, got dressed and after second thoughts, I put the pink pill in my pocket. If I started to have a meltdown I could take the pill, if I was okay, I wouldn't. Seemed like a fair compromise to me.

Linda was definitely watching me like a hawk today. She must be suspicious. Every time I looked up she was watching me. How could she know? She couldn't could she. It was me, I was paranoid wasn't I? Although - these thoughts might be progress. I was recognising that I may be paranoid wasn't I?

I was relieved when I was sent out for the afternoon to pick up a load of supplies from one of the farms that she dealt with. It was a three-hour round-trip and I loved every minute of it. I had the stereo up full blast, singing my heart out and tapping my seven fingers on the steering wheel. The sun was shining and the birds were singing, I grinned from ear to ear with happiness as I cruised along the B roads. It was a good day to be alive.

Once I had picked up everything that she had requested, I turned back for home. The thought of seeing Linda's beautiful face made me feel so happy, my heart swelled at the thought of my lovely wife who would be waiting for me.

On arriving back at the garden centre I tried my best to fix my face into its previous numb state. I didn't want her to be suspicious of me; after all I hadn't done any harm.

"Did everything go okay?" She asked as I came in carrying a crate full of potatoes.

"Everything was fine." I said as robotically as I could.

"Could you hold the fort here if I just pop out for a minute?"

"Yes."

She smiled and then left, while I carried on unloading potatoes from the van.

The next bit is a bit hazy. I remember a flashing light, then a loud high pitched noise that dropped me to my knees. Then the next thing I remembered was waking up on the couch at home.

"Where the hell have you been?" Linda was asking me as I opened my eyes.

I looked around me in shock. "How did I get here?" I was puzzled.

"You tell me. I left you unloading potatoes two hours ago. You left without locking up. We could have been robbed or anything. Why did you come home?"

I stared at her confused. "The last thing I remember was unloading potatoes."

She sat down at the side of me on the couch, her face pretty face ashen. "Please don't tell me you've had a blackout."

I thought hard trying to recall anything about how I got home. I shook my head. "I don't know."

She looked down at my hands, the last trace of colour draining from her face. "Is that blood yours?"

Chapter Five

The following day I didn't dare take any chances and took the pink pill. Strangely though, it didn't seem to numb me quite as much as usual. Perhaps because it had been out of my system for a few days. Originally it had taken three months to get into my system properly.

I didn't dare risk another black out, god knows what the hell I had done the day before. I could still see a trace of blood under my finger nails.

I stayed home as Linda wasn't sure I should be around the public just in case it happened again. I wish I hadn't after what I saw on the news.

'Police have found the body of Elaine Logan who was reported missing last night. Police have just confirmed that her mutilated body was found in a ditch near her home this morning.'

No.

I felt my heart plummet into my stomach as the news team flashed up a photo of the girl who slipped her phone number into my pocket a few days earlier.

No.

I couldn't do something like that. I shook my head. No. It wasn't me. It probably wasn't the same girl, most young woman look the same nowadays. They all emulate the same style don't they?

I went through the laundry basket pulling out all of the dirty clothes until I found the pair of jeans I was wearing a few days previous. I slid my hand into the back pocket and pulled out the folded-up piece of paper that was still there. Unfolding it I paled at the name scrawled above the phone number. *'Elaine, call me.'*

I screwed it up. Once my panic had subsided, I took it outside and burnt it with a match. There. That made me feel much better. Out of sight, out of mind.

I have no memory of speaking to her other than that day at work. I wouldn't hurt anybody, let alone a woman. I scoffed at the idea. How could I think I could do such a thing, even for a brief second?

Humming to myself I got on with making Linda something nice to eat for dinner.

The day after the dead girl was found, I had to go and see Dr Patel again. After much debate with myself I decided to go sans pink pill. This would be strange. I was curious; would I be able to fool the Doctor as I did my wife? Although in all honesty I wasn't sure if she did suspect. She was watching me like a hawk lately, probably because of the blackout I supposed.

"Should I tell Dr Patel about the blackout?" I had asked her.

"In light of the blood on your hands, no. It could be a one off, let's not jump to conclusion just yet."

So once again I found myself sitting in the waiting room at the hospital tapping my fingers impatiently.

"Crap in here isn't it." A young man on my right said.

This was new; no one had ever spoken to me here before.

"Yeah rubbish isn't it." I agreed looking at him sideways. He looked around eighteen or nineteen. Short dark hair and dark eyes. Quite pretty for a boy.

"The name's Sid." He volunteered.

"Flynn." I returned.

"Cool name."

"Thanks. My parents had a sense of humour. My last names Locke, but my middle name's Thomas."

He thought about it for a little while before laughing. "Flynn T Locke. That's a gun isn't it?" He slapped his knee laughing. He was obviously easily amused.

I smiled back. "Yeah my Dad was a gun enthusiast."

"Cool." He smiled back at me. "So what are you in for?"

"Left frontal lobe syndrome. You?"

"I'm a schizo. So my other self tells me."

"They say I was a bit schizo after my head injury."

"I thought you looked interesting. I think we're just further up the evolutionary ladder than most people. After all, our bodies have evolved to hold multiple personalities." He paused. "Let me ask you something Flintlock, do you think our multiple personalities have their own souls?"

That wasn't anything that had ever occurred to me. Was the 'other one' a proper soul?

"I really hadn't thought of it like that." I replied. "There's only one 'other' and I normally don't have a clue that he's visited. Although I do dream that I'm talking to him. Why? Do you think they have souls?"

"I do."

I was intrigued. "Do you remember anything that 'they' do?"

"Bits and pieces. But mostly not. Although I dream about them too."

"You do? Where are you in the dream?" I was getting so excited that I was forgetting my mask of numbness. I remembered just in time before I was called to Dr Patel's office.

"To be continued." I said to Sid as I left.

He saluted me in agreement.

"Hello Flynn. How are you today?" Dr Patel shook my hand and beckoned me to sit down.

"I'm fine." I replied calmly.

He looked up at me with amusement. "Fine." He paused. "I have been doing a little research since last time we met, and I wonder about trying a new drug. Instead of the anti-psychotic risperidone, I'd like to try you on an anti-depressant. Obviously I'm not going to just take you off risperidone; you've been on it too long to just stop the drug. However I intend weaning you off it and onto the new one, citalopram."

This was unexpected. "What would happen if I just stopped taking the risperidone?"

He leaned back in his seat and crossed his legs. "If you just stopped taking a drug like risperidone, you would experience very strong mood swings, much worse than what you had before. You could become delusional, aggressive, possibly to a psychotic degree."

I swallowed and tried not to look nervous.

"Don't concern yourself Flynn. None of that will happen. We'll wean you down very gradually, as we wean you onto the new drug. Trust me you will be much better on citalopram. It will level out your moods, without the numbness that you have been describing."

"I think that would be a good thing then." I replied.

"Here, take this to the pharmacy." He said handing me a prescription. "And this." He said handing me an A4 sheet of paper, with almost illegible scrawls on it. "It explains how much of each tablet you should now start taking. I suggest you ask Linda to help you with the new dose." He smiled at me. "Any questions?"

I thought about it. "Just one. Who's that Sid fella' that's in the waiting room?"

He frowned. "I'm not familiar with that patient. But, as you understand, I cannot discuss another patient with you."

"I understand."

"One more thing, have you had an appointment through for the brain scan yet?"

I shook my head.

"I'll chase that up before we meet again next week. Very well, nice to see you Flynn, I'll see you again next week."

I stood up. I was dismissed.

Off I went back to the waiting room to wait for Sid.

Chapter Six

I didn't have long to wait. Ten minutes perhaps before I saw him walking towards me.

"Do you want to resume?" He asked mysteriously.

"I do."

"Then let me lead the way." He grinned.

I complied and followed after my new friend.

"Where are we going? I asked.

"Cafeteria here does good coffee and muffins." He called behind him without slowing down.

"Oh, okay."

We went through the big pair of glass doors and into the café. The smell of coffee and fresh baked muffins hit my stomach like a sharp blow. I took a deep breath to savour the smell.

We joined the queue and bought cappuccino and chocolate chip muffins, before taking them back to a table. I noticed with delight that Sid had picked the corner table away from everyone else. Good. I wouldn't have to worry about people sitting behind me.

We sat in companionable silence for a while eating our muffins. Once we had both finished I asked him. "Which Doctor do you see?"

"Dr Hopkins. Which do you see?"

"Dr Patel."

"Ah the new guy. What's he like?" He took a swig of coffee.

"Quite nice actually. Seems to care anyway."

"Makes a change." He seemed quite cynical for one so young.

Enough with the small talk, I got down to business. "What did you mean earlier when you said you dream about your 'other personalities'?"

He raised his eyebrows. "Just what I said. I dream about them, quite a lot actually."

"Do they all look like you?"

"No." He shook his head.

This was unexpected I thought he would be like me, seeing a different version of himself. "What do they look like then?"

"There's three of them. One looks just like my dad, but meaner. He's called Pat. There's a kid called Bobby, he's got the most awful stutter you ever heard. Then there's a sort of devil man, I just call him the devil."

I looked at him closely. He was way crazier than me.

He stared right back at me. "Come on then Flynn, share with the class."

"Okay, I've just got the one; I call him the 'other one'. He looks just like me when I dream about him. We're always on a bus when I'm talking to him. I don't like him, he's scary."

"You're on a bus when you dream? Every dream?"

I nodded. "How about you? Where are your dreams?"

"I'm always in my bedroom from when I was a kid."

"Oh." I thought for a while as I finished my cappuccino. "What did you mean earlier about our other personalities having souls?"

"What it says on the tin. I mean, who's to say if there is only one soul inside my body that it belongs to me? Might be Bobby's for all I know."

"Goodness I hadn't thought of it like that. What if 'other me' is the one with the soul. What if I'm just a figment of his imagination?"

"How do I know I'm not talking to him right now?" He nodded at me.

This was a real head scratcher.

I went back home after exchanging phone numbers with my new friend. He had an interesting perspective.

Linda wouldn't be home for a while yet, so I switched the TV on and sat down. I watched the news for a little while before I got bored and started channel flicking. Another woman was missing apparently.

Absolutely categorically nothing to do with me! I only had the one black out.

I quickly put the thought of missing women out of my head, and switched the channel to Countdown.

I started to drift into my own thoughts as *Rachel Riley* failed to keep my attention. What if Sid had been right? What if I was the 'other'? Maybe 'other one' was the real one. Shit, I thought, if he's the real one I better at least ask him his name the next time I saw him.

I suddenly became aware of the folded-up paper that was digging into my leg through my trousers. I pulled it out. It was the prescription for the new medication and the instructions for weaning off the pink pill. I screwed it up and put it in the bin. I didn't need it; I was doing fine on my own.

Linda arrived home looking tired and worried. She gave me a sad smile as she came into the kitchen. "How did you get on at hospital?"

"Fine. The usual. Dr Patel said he's going to chase up the brain scan." I didn't want to mention the medication change.

"That's good." She sounded distracted.

"How was your day?" I tried to keep the worry off my face.

"Not good." Her lip started to wobble as she sat down on the chair at the head of the kitchen table.

I put my arms around her shoulders. "Tell me what's happened."

She rubbed at my hands that were rested on her shoulders. "It's my dad. I just got a call from my cousin Josie to say that my dad's been taken into hospital with a suspected heart attack. I'm going to have to go." She looked up at me with eyes full of tears.

"You should go." I said decisively. "I'll hold the fort here for a few days while you're gone."

She dried her eyes on the sleeve of her jumper. "Could you cope though?"

"I think so." I didn't see any reason why not.

"I'll close the garden centre for a few days if you can just go and water up and keep an eye on things?" She was looking a little better now I thought.

"Fine." Actually, I was relieved. I was on the verge of panicking about dealing with customers, but just watering up and keeping an eye on things would be okay.

"Do you mind if I go pack a few things and set straight off?"

I shook my head. "Not at all. Go. I'll be fine."

"Sure?"

"Yes go."

She packed and went.

This would be interesting, home alone. Home alone, with no pink pill.

Once she was safely out of the way, I turned Linda's iPod on - after fathoming how the bloody thing worked. I put it on the little speaker dock-thingy and turned it up full blast.

It was great, I hadn't danced in years and certainly never with as much abandon as I was giving it this time. When *The Clash* came on I started pogoing, I forgot how much I loved *The Clash*. I gave myself over completely *to 'Should I stay or should I go'*.

Next came *Blondie*. I always fancied *Deborah Harry*. I danced away all through the *Parallel Lines album*. By the time *Elvis* came on I was gyrating my hips and doing the *Elvis* sneer. I looked up when I saw movement out of the corner of my eye. My next-door neighbour was watching me through the window and gesturing at me to turn the music down. Whoops, I had just been in the middle of jumping off the couch like *Elvis* did off the stairs in the *Jailhouse Rock* Video.

"Sorry!" I mouthed rushing across the room to turn the iPod down.

The old dear from next door glared at me and left.

I hoped she wouldn't tell Linda. If she did, I'd have to deny it, say the old dear was going senile or something. If Linda found out I had been singing and dancing the charade would be over.

But, Linda wasn't here, and didn't know yet, so I would enjoy it while I still could.

I trooped off to find my old headphones, then I could blast my eardrums to my heart's content. I eventually found a pair in the kitchen drawer. Brilliant, I beamed to myself as I popped them into my ears, now my night was set.

Next on my playlist was the greatest hits of *The Rolling Stones*. Okay if I was going to be doing an impression of *Mick Jagger* I would need a microphone. Back I went to the kitchen. After rummaging through the drawers I found my perfect microphone -a nice wooden spoon to sing into.

Chapter Seven

That night I fell asleep happy. I spoke briefly on the phone to Linda just before bed. Her dad was still very poorly but stable. She wanted to know if I would be okay for another few days, while she stayed on to look after him.

"No problem at all." I told her.

Truth was, I was enjoying myself. I did feel a little guilty about how upset Linda was - and for my poor father-in-law, but the novelty of feeling so alive was too intoxicating to dwell on the guilt for long.

I lay in bed, diagonally taking up the whole bed and smiling to myself. I didn't last long before my eyelids got heavy.

I opened my eyes into the pitch black and strained my ears at the strange noise that had woken me up. I reached over to Linda to wake her, feeling over a bundle of blankets. I started to panic as my hand couldn't find her. "Linda." I hissed. "Linda. There's someone in the house."

I strained my ears and listened intently again. I could definitely hear something downstairs. "Linda!" In desperation, I leaned over to her side of the bed and switched on the lamp. The bulb had gone in the lamp on my side about six months ago and I never got around to changing it. Light. But no Linda. I'd forgotten for a minute that she wasn't here. Oh god! I put my hands over my face.

"What do I do?" I whispered to myself.

I was panting with fear as I got out of bed and looked around desperately for something to use as a weapon. I was cursing Linda for taking away the carving knife I had wanted to keep under my pillow. The only thing I could find to hand was a candlestick from off the window ledge. With shaking hands and trembling knees I slowly opened the bedroom door and listened. All was quiet for a moment, and then I heard it. Two voices talking quietly together. I panicked and crept back into the bedroom and shut the door. My god there were two of them! I was panting and starting to cry as I shoved the dressing table up against the door. There. Hopefully that should keep the burglars out while I had chance to think.

I was crying as I slid under the bed to hide.

I lay there for around twenty-minutes in terror listening to the faint voices down there before I realised that I recognised the voices. I strained a bit more to hear, before realising that I was listening to *The Good Life*. I had gone to bed without turning the TV off.

I slid out from under the bed feeling foolish for mistaking *Tom and Barbara Good* for burglars. I let out a huge sigh of relief and wiped the tears from my eyes with the back of my hands. I moved the dressing table out of the way of the door and went downstairs, to watch the rest of *The Good Life.*

I must have fallen asleep watching it, as I woke up the next morning on the couch with cramp.

Linda called me early, to check on me I think. "How are you coping on your own?"

"I'm fine." I lied. I would have crossed my fingers as I lied to her, but I was holding the phone with my right hand, and it was difficult to cross the fingers on my left hand, as I only had a thumb and a little finger.

"I'll be here till day after tomorrow if that's okay with you?" She continued.

"Fine. How's your dad doing?"

She sighed what sounded like a sigh of relief. "He's doing a lot better. He can go home tomorrow. I want to go with him and get him settled, then I'll come back the day after when his nurse starts." She paused before saying. "I have to go; a doctor wants to talk to me. I miss you."

"I miss you too." I really did.

"Bye love."

"Bye Linda."

I hung up and went off to start my usual routine. Got dressed, got washed, threw pink pill away. There, back in a routine, that was much better.

I was just heading into work when my phone started beeping to tell me I had a text. I unlocked the main door and went straight into the office. Pulling the phone out of my pocket I saw I had a text from my new friend Sid, or maybe one of his 'others'.

Hey Flintlock,
Ya Busy?
Sid

I smiled. It was nice to have a mate. I text him straight back.

Hi Sid,
Not busy, just doing a few jobs at the wife's garden
centre.

Not a minute passed before he text me back.

Need Any Company? I'm Bored shitless.

I smiled and sent him the address. I left the front door unlocked but with the closed sign on and began watering all of the plants as I had promised Linda I would do.

I was probably three-quarters through it when I heard the front door open.

"Hiya!" Sid called over to me.

"Hey Sid, I won't be a minute with this. If you want to go through there to the office there's a kettle if you want to make a coffee." I gestured off towards the far side.

"Great I'm parched. Have you got tea bags though, I'm more of a tea person?"

"Sure there's some on top of the fridge."

"Cool. Do you want one making?" He turned back.

"Yeah I'll have a tea for a change. Milk two sugars ta."

He disappeared off into the office.

Once I'd finished watering the last of the Begonias, I joined him in the office. It was a bit of a stretch to call it an office really, more like a walk in cupboard with two cramped chairs. Sid was just stirring the teas when I came in.

"There you go Flynn, tea, milk with two sugars." He slid it over to me.

"Thank you very much." I picked up the cup carefully as it was very full. "We'll go have this out in the back greenhouse, it's lovely and warm in there, and it looks out over the fields."

I led the way through the main greenhouse that held all the annuals, through the middle room that held the perennials and out to the last greenhouse where all the fruit and orchids were. I loved it in this greenhouse, the views out of the window and the smells from the flowers wafting in were amazing.

There was a pile of straw bales piled up against the far side, so I led the way over to them; they made a most comfortable seat. We sat side by side facing the midday sun high over the fields of corn visible through the greenhouse windows. We got comfortable lounging out on the straw with our cups of tea.

Sid seemed a little more subdued then the last time I saw him. After sitting in an awkward silence for a while I decided to break the ice. "So, what's up then Sid?"

He shrugged. "Nothing really, just feeling a little, what's the word?" He looked up as if for an answer. "Despondent. I think that's the word. I'm not getting on that great with my mum, my step-dad think's I'm a loser and I just had a row with my sister. So I thought fuck 'em, I'd get out for a bit."

I was amused but pretending to be sympathetic. "What was the row with your sister about?"

He rolled his eyes. "She accused me of stealing her boyfriend's LSD. Her boyfriend's a dealer and apparently he stashed a load of shit at our house. Now it's gone. But she's been filling the house with junkies for the last two days, so what does she expect really? That they won't go through her room and steal shit?"

"Is your sister a junkie?" I was curious; I have never had any experience with drugs. Well apart from cannabis when I was at Uni but that doesn't count.

"No she's okay mostly. Just the odd joint and bit of wiz. It's her bloke that's the shit-head."

I didn't really know what to say. In the end I just said what came natural. "So what's the deal with being schizo then? How's that working out for you?"

He sniggered, and looked sideways at me.

"Wow takes a nutter to know a nutter you know. Tell me your shit and I'll tell you mine."

I thought that was a fair enough deal.

"I was on a bus that got blown up by a suicide bomber. Got brain-damaged, went a bit psychotic for a few years. You know, the usual."

"Oh yeah that sounds very usual." He laughed nervously. "Is that how you lost your fingers?"

"Yep, and my sanity."

"Sanity's over rated."

"I quite agree." I grinned. "Come on then, what's your deal?"

He looked a little uncomfortable.

"I went through a trauma when I was little. When I started acting out, at first everyone thought I had ADHD, but I just got worse and worse. By the time I turned fourteen I had a psychotic breakdown and tried to kill my teacher. So they say anyway. I don't really remember it. I've had a few little episodes since then, but mostly I'm okay -as long as I take the little pink tablet anyway."

I nearly spilt my tea with excitement. "You have the little pink pill? Not risperidone?"

"Yeah, why is that what you have?"

"Yes! Well I did, do, did." Hell I was confusing myself. "Do you find it numbs you? Turns you into an emotionless robot?" I was leaning towards him with eagerness, spilling tea all over his trainers.

He looked down at his tea covered shoes but didn't seem bothered. "I know what you mean, about the numbness." He nodded.

"I can't bear the numbness. In fact, can I tell you a secret?"

"Shoot." He shrugged. "Who would believe me anyway?"

"True." I paused. "I've stopped taking the pink pill. But no one can know, just you and me. I can't believe how good it is to feel again. I've been so numb for so long, but now I feel so alive!" I threw my hands in the air laughing.

He looked at me and started laughing. I grinned back.

"Okay." He said. "You've told me your secret, let me tell you mine." He put his cup down on the floor. "I've found a way to keep taking the pink pill, but still feel the most amazing things you could ever imagine."

"How?"

He dug in his coat pocket and pulled out an envelope. "Let me introduce you to my little friend LSD." He winked.

Chapter Eight

"So you did take her LSD?" I was shocked.

"Well, if you can't be honest with your mates what's the fucking point?"

I couldn't really argue with his logic.

"Ever dropped acid?" He asked giving me an assessing look.

"Nope."

"Never?" He asked incredulously. "But wasn't you around in the swinging sixties when everybody was on the stuff?"

"I'm not that bloody old!"

"How old? When were you born?"

"Why do you want to see my ID?" I laughed. "I'm forty. Born in '74. How about you?"

"Forty? Man that's old." He shook his head giving me a sly smile. "I'm twenty-four."

"No way. You can't be more than nineteen at a push."

He seemed insulted. "Do you want some acid or what?"

"I don't know." I shrugged. "Do I?"

"Hell yeah." He started taking out of his envelope a little plastic bag with what looked like little squares of paper in it."

"Is that it?" I was very curious.

"Yep. And this." He said pulling out a bottle of pills from his pocket. "This is diazepam." He held up the little brown bottle. "This is what you take if you freak out and want to stop the trip."

I scratched my head. I didn't really know what to do. I've never been good with moral dilemmas. "How do you take it? Just swallow it?"

"You place it on your tongue and let it melt. It doesn't take long."

He held out to me the little square of paper on the tip of his index finger. He gestured with his eyes from mine to the little square paper.

Hell I never claimed to be good with peer pressure. I took it and put it straight on my tongue.

"There you go." He laughed and clapped before putting his own little square of paper on his tongue.

After that we clicked our cups of tea together, and I said "Bottoms up."

He said "You mean Queers, ma Dear's," and sniggered.

We finished our teas and waited.

We sat chatting for about ten minutes or so about this and that, all the while I'm thinking at the back of my mind, 'Jesus Christ I just took acid!'

I suddenly realised that Sid had stopped talking. I looked up to ask him why he'd stopped when I realised that he was still talking, he'd just been slowed down so much that I could barely see his lips moving. It was like he had been switched into slow-play mode. I was fascinated!

Every gesture I made was like lightening. I watched with delight when my right arm turned into a lightsaber like off *Star Wars*. I moved it up and down and side to side as it lit up and went - "Shum, shum." I giggled with delight. "Sid!" I yelled at him. "Speed up."

As I watched him it looked like someone had switched him onto fast forward by remote control. Eventually he reached the same speed as me.

"Sid look at my arm. It's a lightsaber." I waved at him again. He laughed and looked down at his own arm. I exclaimed. "Holy shit! You've got one too!"

"So I have!" He laughed and charged me.

We played for a while swiping at each other our lightsaber arms.

"This is so much fun!" I giggled as I fell over the straw bale backwards. Wow, from down here the sun light was amazing. I could see each individual sunbeam separating and dropping to the floor like golden droplets of rain. I wondered what the raindrops would taste like? Bitter apparently. The golden rain was Sid urinating onto what he thought was a urinal.

I blinked at the bitter sunbeams and started laughing. I crawled across the floor on my hands and knees still giggling at the sunbeams that were trying to chase me as I out-crawled them. Finally I got to my feet. There. I'd beaten them.

A section of Petunias turned their heads to watch me with interest.

"Sid!" I exclaimed as I suddenly saw that he was back from wherever he'd been. "I think I'm...I'mmmm...what?"

"What?" He replied.

"Why did you what?"

"What?" He started laughing again, closely followed by me.

We held each other up laughing until our cheeks were hurting. I looked up suddenly and pointed. "Is that here for us?" I was puzzled.

"What? Is what here for us?" He sounded confused.

"That big red bus there." I pointed. "Come on Sid, let's go get on the bus." I dragged him over to the side door as it opened.

"Where did this come from?" He asked climbing aboard the bus.

"I think it's here for us."

I climbed up after him and nodded to the driver. He doffed his cap at us. I followed Sid down the aisle to the back of the bus.

"Sid, we're on my bus! My bus where the 'other one' is."

He started laughing, holding his belly and stamping his feet. "We're in your fucking head!"

I put both hands to my head in shock. "No!" I felt the size of my head with my hands. "A bus couldn't fit in there."

Sid started laughing at my serious face. I didn't know why he was laughing at me. I turned away from him thinking to myself, 'he's as high as a kite.'

I noticed 'other me' watching us with amusement from the other side of the bus. I elbowed Sid without taking my eyes off 'other me'. "Sid." I elbowed him. "Sid!" I elbowed him again. "Look! Over there! 'Other me's here."

"Where?" He looked puzzled.

"There!" I pointed to the seat opposite.

"Shit that's trippy." He said with amazement looking from me to 'other me'. "What does he want?"

"I don't know." I stared at 'other me' who just stared back at me with amusement. "Hey if he's here are your 'other's' here?"

"Fuck!" He looked around him in horror. "Oh shit, duck!"

I ducked. "Who is it?" I hissed.

"It's bloody stuttering Bobby."

"BBBBBobby?" I asked laughing. "BBBBobbbby." I liked how it sounded.

I climbed back up into my seat, ignoring 'other me' who was still eyeballing me. I looked around but I couldn't see Bobby. I leaned my head down to Sid. "It's okay, he's gone."

"It's okay, I'm gonna stay down here for a while, this bus mattress is comfy." He curled up into the foetal position smiling and sucking his thumb.

I sat in my seat staring at 'other one', who was staring back at me. It suddenly dawned on me, I had meant to ask him something the next time I saw him. I leant forward in my seat to address him and fell over.

Never mind, this bus mattress was very comfy. I'd ask him his name next time.

Chapter Nine

I woke up a while later with my heart beat thundering in my ears like a drum. I opened my eyes and found that I was laid across a bay of crushed marigolds. As I sat up I felt a sharp pain in my head. I felt the back of my head to find that I had a wooden plant-label stuck there. I pulled it out wincing. I was a little confused. Wasn't I just on a bus? With Sid?

"Sid?" I shouted, looking around me.

I got up and stepped out of the crushed marigold patch; I dusted my jeans down and walked up the path towards the last greenhouse where I last remembered seeing him.

"Sid! Sid! Where are you?" I was starting to panic now. Oh my god I had just taken acid with someone that I hardly knew! Scrap that, I had just taken a class A drug with a certified schizophrenic, who has previously tried to kill his teacher!

Oh my god, oh my god, oh my god!

I put my hands on top of my head and looked around desperately for Sid. An awful thought struck me. "What if Sid isn't real?"

I sat down on the floor crossed legged and tried to subside my panic attack. I was panting with fear and my heart rate had gone through the roof. I was the only person that had seen Sid wasn't I? When I asked Dr Patel about Sid he said he'd never heard of him! Oh my god he was another 'other' wasn't he? I started rocking trying to sooth myself. I tried to reason with myself. If Sid didn't exist where the hell had I got LSD from? I didn't know anyone who *did* drugs let alone sold them. I was just trying to puzzle where I could have got it from when Sid stepped out from the office carrying two cups of tea.

'Others' couldn't carry real cups could they? I was stumped.

He handed me a cup of tea. It burnt my fingers it was so hot. That cup of tea was definitely real, so, the man who made it must be real. I was so relieved I nearly cried. I wasn't that crazy after all.

"Sid!" I cried with relief.

"That's my name." He said sitting down across from me, putting his cup down on the floor carefully so as not to spill it. "What did you think then?" He asked me looking curious.

What did I think? I wasn't sure. "Did all that really happen? The lightsabers, and the bus?"

"Did it feel like it happened?"

"It felt so real. You were on my bus."

"I was. It was pretty intense for a while there."

"Did you see my 'other'?"

"I really did." He laughed with surprise and shook his head. "He was sitting across from us watching us. He looked just like you."

"That's amazing. I can't believe you were on my bus." I paused remembering. "With Bobby! You were on the bus with Bobby!"

"Oh yeah I forgot about that." He picked up his tea and had a long slurp. "By the way, sorry for peeing on you."

"What?"

"I thought you were a urinal for a while back there."

I looked down, my clothes were a little damp, and I could faintly smell urine. I felt quite surreal and philosophical. "Well if you can't pee on your mates, who can you pee on?"

"Can't argue with that!"

Once we'd finished our tea and describing our version of events to each other, we each went our separate ways. Sid went off to go to a friend's house, while I went home.

I shouldn't have driven really, although the acid trip had stopped, my perception was still a little *off.* I was relieved to get home in one piece.

Once I was home I dug the prescription for the new tablets out of the bin. I would be good from now on. I would be a model husband and patient. No more taking illegal drugs with schizophrenics, no more fooling around not taking my medication. Dr Patel had told me the new tablets would stop me from being numb all the time once I was weaned onto them. So I would give them a chance. In the meantime though, I took three little pink pills, hopefully that should replace the ones I should have been taking.

After that, I peeled my stinking wet-clothes off and put them in the washer while I went off for a soak in the bath.

I ran it to just the right temperature and thought I would treat myself by indulging in Linda's best bubble bath. I think I must have put too much in, when I came back into the bathroom from getting my dressing gown out of the bedroom, they were overflowing over the side of the bath like a white frothy water monster.

"Shit!" I panicked and started pulling armfuls of bubbles off the top and tried to put in into the sink to get rid of it. But the bubbles kept on growing!

I pulled up another armful off the carpet and flicked the toilet seat up with my big toe and tried to drop the bubbles in the toilet. I wiped my soap-sudded hands on my bare legs and pressed the button on the top of the toilet to flush the bubbles away.

"Oh no!" I cried as the bubbles burst over the side of the toilet.

"What to do?" I asked myself in the mirror.

The bastard winked back at me and said "Hide them under the bed."

I stared at him in amazement for a moment before replying. "Good idea."

I got a bath towel off the radiator and started scooping bubbles off the top of the bath before they could fall onto the floor and dropped them onto the towel. I had a pretty good pile there I thought, so I dragged the towel full of bubbles along the landing to my bedroom, where I managed to pull the towel of bubbles under the bed. I pulled the quilt-cover over the side of the bed to hide the mess. I stood up with relief. "Good. That's that taken care of. Just the toilet to empty of bubbles now."

I trekked back into the bathroom to find a bath that was completely empty, no bubbles, no water.

"Shit!" What the hell was going on? I went over to the mirror to ask 'other me' what was going on. He was still there laughing at me. "What's going on?" I demanded. "Where's the bubbles gone?" I pointed my finger at him accusingly, but he pointed his right back at me.

"There were no bubbles or water in the bath. You're still tripping."

"I am?" Was he winding me up?

I went to sit down on the toilet seat to think about it but I'd forgotten I'd lifted the lid earlier, so I fell through. The cold water on my bum woke me up with a start.

It was all too much, I decided to go to bed and sleep it off, I'd be better tomorrow I was sure.

I was worried about Tom and Barbara Good burgling me again so I decided to hide and sleep under the bed with the bubbles so that they wouldn't find me if they ransacked the bedroom.

Chapter Ten

The next morning I awoke wondering where in the hell I was. I sat straight up and banged my head on the mattress lattes above me. "Ow." I rubbed my sore head. Realising where I was, I slid out from under the bed dragging a towel out from under there that I must have been using as a pillow.

I couldn't really take in all that had happened the previous day. I couldn't differentiate between what was real and what wasn't. One thing was certain though; by the smell of urine on my clothes, I definitely hadn't had a bath! I made that my first priority.

Whilst running the water into the bath tub I had a brief recollection about a bubble monster. Never mind. I shook my head to try and rid it of the memory.

Once I was clean and into fresh clothes I felt much better.

I looked closely at my reflection in the mirror as I brushed my teeth. "Did I really see 'other me' in you last night?" I asked him.

He just stared at me with a toothbrush hanging out of his mouth, so I decided to go and get the kettle on.

Once I was in the kitchen with a cup of coffee in hand, I noticed that I must have taken my prescription for the lower dose risperidone and the new drug citalopram out of the bin.

"Why would I do that?" I questioned myself. "I don't want to be numb again." I screwed it up in a ball and tossed it into the bin. "Goal!" I shouted as it landed safely in the net.

The phone began to ring deafeningly loud from the wall next to the fridge. I cringed at the sound; it was much louder than normal.

"Hello?"

"Flynn? How are you? Are you coping okay?" It was Linda.

I was delighted to hear from her but managed to rein it in before answering. "Hi Linda, I'm fine. How are you? Oh and how's your dad?" That sounded good I thought.

"I'm a lot better for hearing your voice." She sounded like she was smiling as she was speaking. "Dad's much better now, it's such a relief."

"That's great. I'm glad."

"He's coming home today, I'm going to stay on and keep an eye on him till his new nurse starts tomorrow. A male nurse to Dad's disappointment! He was looking forward to the bed baths, should have seen his face when he found out it would be a man doing them!" She laughed.

I loved her laugh, and smiled at hearing it. "Well don't worry about anything here, I'm fine, and so is the garden centre."

"I can't believe how well you've done Flynn. I'm so proud of you for coping in a crisis like this."

"All thanks to you Linda." Oh shit I nearly started crying there. Better wrap this up quick before I give the game away. "Linda, there's someone at the door, I better go."

"Okay love, well I'll see you tomorrow morning anyway."

"Can't wait. Bye."

"Bye."

I put the receiver down with a thud. God I would have to get better at masking these emotions before she got back tomorrow.

After some breakfast I decided to go into work and water up. I picked my car keys up off the counter-top lovingly and twirled them around my finger. I loved being able to drive again. I lost my license for years after the head injury; I only got it back last year after taking a re-test. Plus my old doctor, Dr Mandela had vouched for me after I'd done so well with the risperidone.

I let myself out of the back door and walked down the gravel drive towards my parking space. The noise the gravel was making was annoying me greatly today. It sounded like walking across cornflakes or something. I shook my head, this was no good, we'd have to get tarmac.

I was a little disturbed to find that someone must have been messing about with my van since I left it. Someone must have broken into it and disengaged the handbrake as the van was now resting in the hedgerow in my front garden.

"What the hell?" I went rushing over to it to assess the damage.

"Bastards!" I bellowed at the top of my voice. Both wing mirrors were missing and there was a large scratch down the front of the bonnet, worse than that though was the clump of hair that was hanging off my front bumper. I stepped closer for a better look. "Ugh!" I stepped back quickly. There was a piece of bloody skin around the size of a fifty-pence-piece stuck to the bumper with a patch of long dark hair hanging off it.

I didn't know what to do.

I went back into the house and sat down on the lino to think. Someone must've taken my van. That must be it. If I'd done that to the van I would remember it. How could I think even for a second that I could have done that?

I'm an excellent driver.

After giving it much thought I decided it was definitely joyriders. I briefly thought about reporting the crime to the police but thought better of it as my insurance premiums were already sky high. No, I'd fix this myself.

I jet-washed the blood and hair off the bumper, feeling sorry for whoever's dog must have been run over. That was long hair, must've been an afghan or something like that.

Once the van was clean again and out of the hedgerow I felt better. I'd go to work and water up as planned, then I would go to the scrap yard and buy two new wing mirrors for the van.

I got to work to find everything there was fine. All that seemed wrong was the patch of marigolds that looked crushed in one of the bays. I got on with the mammoth task of watering all the plants and shrubs, all the time though my eyes kept wandering back to the patch of crushed marigolds. What excuse could I give Linda as to what had happened to them? I could hardly tell her me and my schizophrenic mate passed out on them whilst taking LSD.

"Shit!" I announced to myself. Linda would take one look at those mangled flowers and know what I had done. She'd see it on my face. She'd know about everything. The lies, the drugs, the spitting out of the pink pill. "My god she's going to leave me!"

My attention wandered from what I was supposed to be doing and I accidently sprayed the power sockets with water. "NO, no, no, no, no!" I turned the hose the other way instead and soaked myself. Eventually I managed to turn the hose off. I spluttered and shouted, drying my face off with the handkerchief that I always carry in my pocket. Will the electric sockets still work? I wondered. My god what if I had blown all of the electricity in the place?

"Linda's definitely going to leave me!" I told the socket as I stared at it. "She really is." I started to get a lump in my throat. I slid down to the floor to cry in the puddle I had made with the hose.

After a few minutes of sobbing I told the lobelia that I was sitting next to. - "I don't like feeling things anymore. I can't cope!" I cried.

As the tears started to dry up my vision cleared a bit and I spotted something in amongst the squashed marigolds. I reached over to pull it out to see what it was. "Diazepam." I read off the label of the little brown bottle. "Thank goodness." I looked up at the heavens with relief. I took three and after a little while felt much better.

Once I had calmed down and I was suitably numb, I carefully finished watering up and tidily put the hose pipe away. Next though was to tackle the problems of the marigolds.

The only thing that I could think of to do was to have something 'accidently' fall onto them. Something that I couldn't be blamed for. I looked all around me for something that I could make fall onto them, but I couldn't find a thing that I could make look plausible.

In the end I had to go with gut instinct.

After going up onto the glass roof above - carefully, I broke the pane of glass above the marigolds with a hammer, sending glass shattering down below. Next I dragged a dead tree-branch in from outside and laid it over the mangled marigolds. "There!" I told it with satisfaction. "Now Linda won't leave me."

After finding two second hand wing mirrors at our local scrap yard, I was delighted when for an extra ten pounds each the proprietor would fit them on the spot.

Damn, I was getting good at this problem solving. And, I was supposed to be brain-damaged? I was starting to think not.

Chapter Eleven

I don't think I'd been asleep for long when I woke up on that infernal bus. The smell hit me before I had chance to open my eyes and guess where I was. Why do all buses have that awful dead air, stale cigarette, exhaust fume smell?

I blinked as the orange light burned its way onto my retinas. As my eyes adjusted to the sickly glow I became aware of the other passengers. I looked around at them feeling the panic start to creep up from my stomach. Straight across from me was Elaine, who had given me her telephone number that day. She smiled at me sweetly exposing her bloody-toothless gums. She was wearing a summer dress, blood stained, that stopped short on her torn tights.

Next to her was an angry looking young lady clad in jeans, blouse and gore, who was staring at me with her one remaining dead eye. The other eye was resting on her cheek.

I tore my gaze away from them and looked away to my right, to find 'other one' sitting next to me, his face inches from mine. He smiled his shark like grin at me. He enjoyed my discomfort enormously.

"Where to tonight Flynn?" He peered at me quizzically. "Is tonight the night we go to Daynejonne?"

"Please no. I just want to go home."

"Aw." He mocked me. "Don't be a spoil sport." He leapt up onto the seat with his feet like a frog. "Don't you want to see the bus go boom again?"

"No." I started to cry and closed my eyes.

"Come on…remember what it felt like to be burned by boiled blood?" He laughed like a maniac. "How about when you took your shoe off and a chunk of someone's flesh fell out?" He clapped his hands with delight.

"No. I don't want to remember." I put my fingers in my ears, but my left ones fell off again. "Not again." I screamed as the explosion tore through the bus.

I was so pleased when I woke up the next morning to find that it was Monday, the day that Linda would be back. Thank goodness, it had been hard work coping on my own for the last few days - although I had done a very good job despite many trying obstacles.

I got up, got dressed and took the little pink pill, plus two diazepam for good measure. They had suitably numbed me the day before, so hopefully I won't give the game away to Linda.

I went down stairs and made myself a cup of coffee and some toast, while I waited to go numb. It didn't take that long actually, probably ten minutes or so. Once the tablets kicked in you could have told me I was about to be castrated and I wouldn't have bat an eyelid.

I would have been delighted to see Linda walk through the door, but now I was numb again, so I didn't really care all that much.

"Hey Love!" She beamed at me as she came through the door. "It's good to see you." She gave me a hug.

"You too." I said with little feeling. I put the kettle on to make her a cuppa' while she prattled on for a while about her dad, I don't know what she was on about as I wasn't really listening. I realised suddenly that she might ask me to comment on what she was saying to me, so I tuned in and paid a little more attention.

"I'm not having it. He's not even properly qualified."

What the hell was she talking about? I just nodded and hoped I was nodding and shaking my head in the right places.

She continued regardless. "How can they send someone out to look after a heart-attack patient who doesn't even know how to take someone's blood pressure?"

Ah, it was about the male nurse who would look after her dad.

I made an intelligent comment. "Are you making a complaint about him?"

"Oh yes. I want him gone before he *kills* my father."

"Fair enough."

"So will you?"

Shit what? Kill her dad's nurse? Surly not! Why the hell hadn't I listened to her? I better get her to clarify. "Will I what?"

She looked at me and rolled her eyes. "Will you ask Dr Patel if it is legal for someone with no medical qualifications to become a professional carer?"

"Oh yes of course." Phew!

"When will you see him next?"

"Thursday at 12 o'clock. Or rather whatever time they decide to see me."

"So you will mention it won't you? You won't forget?"

"I won't forget."

"I'd come with you, but I can't afford to take any more time off."

"That's okay; I'll be fine don't worry."

She sat down at the table looking very tired. "I'll just have a quick brew with you and then we'll go into work and open up." She sighed, and put her hands over her face.

I didn't really know what to do, I could see she looked needy I just didn't know if I was expected to do anything. To be on the safe side I patted her on the head as I passed.

Once she was finished with her tea, we went to work together. She always looks nervous when I drive for some reason, I don't know why, I'm an excellent driver. She says I drive too aggressively, but I dispute this. I think I drive with confidence.

I wove in and out of the rush hour traffic with style. When some doddery old bastard tried to cut me up, I got in front of him and slammed on my brakes, see how he liked it.

He didn't, and neither did Linda.

To be honest, Linda was starting to get on my nerves. I didn't like the way she kept staring at me. She looked at me like I was a piece of dirt or something. Who the hell did she think she was? I could also feel the numbness sliding off my brain. Why didn't the risperidone work anymore? Plus the Diazepam didn't seem to last very long.

When Linda started screaming for me to slow down she got on my very last nerve, so I back-handed her as I pulled up to the traffic lights.

Let her blubber. She might think twice about being disrespectful next time.

I was sent home like a naughty child for bad behaviour. Who the hell did Linda think she was? She'd been off gallivanting for days on end leaving me on my own. Then what did I get when she got back? Abuse!

Well, I'm not having it. If she thinks she can treat me like that she can fuck off.

Once I got home I decided to go and have a nap and calm down a bit. I was all on edge after Linda's temper tantrum earlier. I didn't bother getting undressed as I got in bed, I was sure I wouldn't sleep anyway, but it would be nice to be warm and comfortable for a while.

I must have been more tired than I thought, as it wasn't long before I was asleep.

I woke up in a panic. "Oh god no!" I cried out as I shot out of bed. "Please let it be a dream, please let it be a dream!" How could I? How could I hit Linda like that? I *love* Linda, she's my world!

I started to cry as I tried to find the car keys so I could go and tell her how sorry I was. "How did this happen?" I asked myself as I got in the car. "I took the pink pill."

"But you haven't been taking it regularly have you?" 'Other me' commented from the rear-view mirror.

"Go away; I can't be doing with you today!" I told him, and moved the mirror away so that I didn't have to look at him.

I finally got through the busy traffic to the garden centre. I went flying over to the checkout where Linda was serving a customer, arriving out of breath and distraught. I was dying to throw my arms around her and tell her how sorry I was, but I tried to be respectful of the customer she was serving.

I was watching her face closely as she served the man in front of me. She was masking her distress very well I thought, bless her, what a strong courageous woman she was.

I started tearing up again. The lump in my throat made it hard to breath. I was relieved to see that she wasn't bruised from where I hit her; I had visions of her looking like a battered wife.

She looked up at me, still in mid-conversation with the man in front. She looked curiously at me, not fearfully as I had anticipated. I had expected her to cower at my presence I think. Once the man in front had been dealt with he left.

"What are you doing here?" She asked me looking puzzled.

"Linda I'm so sorry I hurt you. I don't know what came over me. I would never ever hurt you, I love you so much." I started properly crying then. I stared down at my feet, watching my tears bouncing off my shoes.

"What's happened?" She asked coming around the counter and putting her arms around me.

I looked up at her in amazement. "How can you bear to touch me? I hurt you?"

"What do you mean you hurt me?"

"I hit you. In the car." I wiped my running nose on the back of my hand.

She looked confused. "No you didn't. You were very quiet in the car but that's all." She wiped my tears away gently. "You said you were tired, so you were going home for a nap. Did you have a nightmare?"

Did I?

"What?" I asked her in confusion.

"You went home for a nap, and said you'd come back later. Oh, Flynn come here." She held me tight and let me sob against her neck for a while. "You must have dreamt it." She kissed my hair.

"I don't dream."

Chapter Twelve

I was okay once I had a cup of tea in the little office. My tears had dried up and I can't tell you how relieved I was that I hadn't hurt Linda. I was certain on arriving I would find her battered and bruised and demanding a divorce. I had also had brief palpitations about her possibly having me arrested and/or committed. It was certainly within her power and quite within reason, I thought.

But no, just a nightmare - that's all it was. Also, I reasoned with myself, I did take LSD the day before. That could have something to do with a distorted sense of reality.

Just then Linda came in. "I forgot to ask you earlier. What happened to the glass roof?" She asked pointing back to the annuals greenhouse.

Ah, I was ready and primed for this one. "A tree branch came down." I said very decidedly.

She screwed up her forehead, puzzled. "I saw the tree branch laid over the marigolds. Trouble is, there isn't a tree within a mile of here. Plus, that tree branch looks remarkably like the piece I had bought to do a display with, out near the entrance."

Whoops. Shit! What now? Come on brain, come up with something. She's looking at you! "Erm, don't know love. Nothing to do with me. It was like that when I got here." Yeah that would have to do.

She didn't look convinced, but she left it alone and got on with arranging for a glazier to come out and repair the broken window.

I sought out my hosepipe and got on with the dreaded task of watering up before I'd have to start pulling out the dead plants to put on the compost heap. As much as I always dreaded watering up, it was okay once I actually got started with it. I think the thought of doing it was much worse than just doing it.

I had a minor panic attack as I reeled the hose out past the electrical point that I had drenched the day before, but that soon past. I noticed Linda had plugged an oscillating fan into it, and unless she was a figment of my imagination, she wasn't dead.

By the time I had got around the entire place I was tired out and dripping with sweat. There was one thing to be said for manual labour, it kept you fit.

I wound the hose back onto the reel, without drenching my shoes this time. (Made a pleasant change.) Once I got my breath back and had stood in front of the fan for a while to cool down, I went to fetch my wheel barrow to throw the dead plants into. It was also my job to 'dead head' the flowers of their old dead blooms to keep them looking nice for display. It was always a back-breaking job that was made even worse by the stifling heat. I slowly worked my way through the annuals, taking care to only throw away the dead flowers - this wasn't always easy as the roots inside the seed trays tended to intertwine with each other. Once upon a time I would have got mad and just thrown the lot away, but today I was being good.

Once my barrow was full, I cautiously made my way through the greenhouses and around the back to the giant compost heap that Linda and I had built. It was huge, but it had to be, we had a hell of a lot of stuff to go in. Linda had told me to put this load in bay number three, as bay number two was too full. I lifted the lid of bay number two to see that she had been right, it was full to the brim. But then again, if I stood in it and jumped up and down I was sure I could flatten it a bit more and fit todays rubbish in it. Why not? I already stank of sweat, a bath would be necessary anyway.

I climbed up over the top and dropped down into the stinking pile with as much force as I could muster. I stomped my feet and was delighted to see that I had made a lot of extra space. My barrow-full would easy fit in now. I gave it one more good stomp down for luck when I spotted something odd. It looked like a piece of blue cloth underneath some squashed leaves. I pealed a handful of leaves back to find a blue-clothed elbow sticking up through the rotting plant matter.

"God no!" I leaped back in horror, almost falling over my feet in an effort to get away from the thing in the bin. I fell back onto the far lip edge and went down with a crash out of the compost bay. I lay there on the ground paralysed with terror, heart bursting with the fear that was cascading through its chambers. I tried to catch my breath but my lungs wouldn't obey, they seemed to be frozen. I thumped at my chest, trying to cry out with breathless panic. I tried to get up off my back and on to all fours, still feeling the paralysed sob trying to burst from my heart. I tried to reason with myself in my head. 'You've got to breathe. You've got to breathe. Take a breath. All it takes is one breath.' I got one breath. Then another, and then another. Panic started to subside as I started to take deep gulps. I dragged myself into sitting position with my back resting against the compost heap. I sat there for an age panting and trying to get myself under control.

Maybe the elbow had been a hallucination? I had one earlier didn't I? I thought I was a wife-beater this morning. Why not think I was a murderer by the afternoon?

I started to relax. It was ridiculous. It was all the LSD talking; I started to laugh a little at my overreaction. Where on earth did my brain come up with this stuff?

Once I was properly calm and back under control, I reached up and closed the lid on bay two without looking back into it. I didn't want to see anymore hallucinations, I had seen more than enough for one day. I opened the lid on the empty bay number three and filled it up with my barrow full of dead flowers.

Four more barrows later and I was finished for the day.

Over the next few days I filled bay number three while ignoring bay number two. I knew there was nothing in there, but still, I didn't want to think about the horrid LSD fuelled vision I had seen. Besides, I had a bigger problem than a false memory of an elbow in a compost bin.
I had run out of risperidone.

On top of that, I had lost the prescription I had been given for the lower dose risperidone and the new pill I was supposed to be taking. I really didn't know what to do. I couldn't tell Linda about the lost prescription, she'd want to know why I hadn't told her about the medication change. And what could I say? 'Sorry love, it would interfere with my experiment.'

She'd say 'what experiment?' Then I would be in deep shit.

So far she hasn't noticed. I've left the old empty box of the pink pill in the kitchen drawer where we keep all of the medication. I'm just praying she doesn't open the box and sees it's empty until I've thought of something.

I'm coping very well though, thanks to Sid's diazepam. The only trouble is that I'm starting to get low on my supply. I think I've got enough to get through until tomorrow, but after that I don't know what I'm going to do.

This afternoon is my appointment with Dr Patel, I'm not looking forward to going, but at least I might see Sid there. I had text him the day before with the excuse of wondering how he was after our 'trip'. It was bullshit though. I was just hoping to bring the conversation around to 'could he score me some more diazepam?' Sadly for me he hadn't replied, so I was banking on seeing him at the hospital so that I could ask him in person.

I was led through to the dreaded waiting room after being weighed again. Why the hell did they have to keep weighing me? I'm not a fucking baby for Christ sake!

Once the nurse had finished irritating me, I was led to the seating area to wait while my time was wasted for a little longer before seeing the doctor that didn't know shit about me anyway.

I was disappointed to find no Sid there in the waiting room. I kicked a chair with disappointment.

Now what?

Chapter Thirteen

"So Flynn? How are you today?" Dr Patel gestured for me to sit down in the chair in front of his desk.

I sat down with a huff, and answered him. "Fine." It came out a little more aggressive than I had intended.

He eyed me with a little suspicion I think. "How have you been since the new medication started? Have you noticed any changes in how you feel, or behave?"

"Not really."

He leaned forward a little, looking at me like he wasn't buying the bullshit I was peddling. "No change at all? No mood swings or sudden outbursts of emotions?"

This wasn't going well. I was overdoing the numb wasn't I? I better give him something to make him leave me alone.

"Well," I began, "I did feel a little anxious for a few days."

"Can you elaborate for me?"

No. "Yes I suppose. Well, actually you asking me to tell you about being anxious is making me anxious." Yep that was good.

"Anxiety." He wrote down in his notes before looking up expectantly. "Anything else?"

"Happiness?"

"You've been feeling happiness?"

"A little."

"That's wonderful." He took his glasses off looking surprised and pleased. "Any negative emotions, anger issues, possibly thoughts about harming yourself, any depression?"

"No. Just a little anxiety that's all."

"I'm delighted to hear that Flynn. It seems you're making real progress here already. I must admit, I thought it might take longer. Risperidone is a difficult drug to wean off from; there can be some major issues for some patients, I'm very glad to hear that you don't seem to be one of them."

"What sort of issues?"

"Some of them have had problems with perception, hallucinations, sometimes delusions. Nothing for you to concern yourself with."

"When do I start the stronger dose of the citalopram?"

"One week today. When you come back in a week's time I will give you the prescription for the stronger dose of citalopram and an even lower dose of risperidone."

Shit. So I had a week to go before I could get a new prescription. "Okay." I nodded.

"I have made some progress with your brain scan, my secretary will be writing to you this week with the exact date and time for it, but it looks like we should be able to squeeze you in sometime before the end of the month."

"Good. Oh, I nearly forgot, my wife wanted me to ask you something. She wanted me to ask, do you know if a professional carer has to have qualifications to be able to work?"

"I'm sorry that's not my area of expertise. Why?"

"Oh. It doesn't matter."

"Before you go, I'd like you to go and see the nurse on reception so that she can get some blood samples from you." He tore off the form he had been filling in. "Please give her this."

I took the form with shaking hands and a stone in my stomach.

"Take care of yourself Flynn and I'll see you at the same time next week." He shook my hand and I was dismissed.

I on the other hand was starting to quietly freak out. I left his office under a cloud of doom. How could I go and get my blood tested? I hadn't been taking the bloody tablets! What would I say next week when he says 'according to your blood tests Mr Locke you haven't been taking your risperidone properly. Plus there was no trace of citalopram in your system. However, we did find huge amounts of diazepam and LSD!'

Fuck fuck fuck fuck fuck!!!!!!!

I hit myself in the side of my head. "What is wrong with me?" I hissed at the carpet.

"Excuse me sir are you okay?" A pretty nurse approached me.

"I'm fine." I lied wiping a bead of sweat off my forehead before it could slide into my eye. With my other hand I was hiding the blood request form behind my back so that she wouldn't see it.

"Do you need help?"

"No, honestly I'm fine. I'm all done here." I started walking away from her, keeping the form out of her field of vision. "Just going home now." I called back to her.

I ran out of the hospital as fast as my legs would carry me.

Once I was sitting behind the steering wheel I let myself go and cried. "How the hell did I get into this mess?" I asked 'other one' who was watching from the rear-view mirror. He didn't answer, he just looked back at me with tear stained puffy eyes. "I've been good for two years. I was on the mend. How has this happened? What do I do?"

No reply.

I could always kill myself. I suddenly thought. No one knows I've gone mad. They would think it was an accident, wouldn't they? If I could make it look convincing.

I was interrupted from this morose train of thought by my phone Bing bonging.

Hey Flintlock
Need a favour. Can u come get me?
118 High St.
Sid

I blew my nose and wrote a reply.

On way now.

I pulled up outside of what I assumed to be Sid's house twenty minutes later. It was a very rough looking street. Most of the houses were boarded up. The ones that weren't didn't look much better. Cardboard boxes and overflowing dust bins seemed to be the main attraction for the thousands of flies that were buzzing around. I stepped over a cat that was fast asleep on the front path of 118 High St. The dirty looking net curtains hung up at the windows did little to help its curb appeal. I carefully stepped around the empty milk bottles and knocked on the red flaky paint that passed for a front door. Straight away one of the dirty curtains was pulled back revealing Sid peering out at me. He gave me the thumbs up and disappeared back behind the curtain.

He came bounding out of the front door sending the empty milk bottles flying like skittles. He charged past me, kicked the cat, and legged it over to my car. He couldn't get in as I had locked it.

I apologised to the disgruntled cat as I followed after him. On getting closer I noted the black eye and the split lip. I blipped the car and said to him. "Get in."

Chapter Fourteen

"Where to then Sid?" I asked starting the engine.

His head was resting against his cut and scratched fist, bruised eyes staring out of the window. "Anywhere."

After another glance at his battered face I decided to head for home. Linda would be at work anyway so I wouldn't have to introduce her to my poor damaged friend. I could sense that he wasn't ready to talk yet, so I didn't try any chit chat, I just got home as fast as I could.

We pulled up into my driveway over the annoyingly noisy gravel and past the damaged hedges that the joyriders had ruined. Mm, I wondered why Linda never mentioned the hedges. She must have noticed them. Perhaps she was trying to be considerate by not quizzing me about it.

"Nice place." Sid observed as he got out of the car.

"Thanks. Come on in, I'll make us a cup of tea."

He followed after me as I headed through the front door and down the hall to the kitchen.

"How the hell did a nutcase like you get a house like this?" He asked incredulously.

I let the insult go. "I got a fair bit of criminal injuries compensation after the accident." I put the kettle on. "Linda thought the safest way to invest the money was in a house. Housing prices always go up don't they?"

"I wouldn't know. Never lived in a private house."

I felt bad. I didn't want Sid to think I was a snob. Far from it, I might live in a detached-house in a nice area now, but I was born and raised in a council house on a pretty rough estate. I hate to think people may mistake me for being privileged. "I've just been lucky, or unlucky depending on how you look at it."

I started pouring the boiling water into the cups while wondering what to say next. I've never been good at small talk. I put his tea in front of him and sat down at the opposite side of the table.

"Thanks." He took the tea cup in his hands gratefully. I quietly observed him from over the brim of my mug as I drank. He looked like he'd been through an ordeal.

He looked up and caught my eye. "Thanks for coming to get me."

"No problem, glad to help. Do you want to talk about it?"

He smirked, "You sound like my therapist."

"Sorry."

"No, I'm sorry. I mean it, thanks for coming to get me. I've had a shitty day to be honest." He rested his head in his hands. "My step-dad caught me with his car this morning and went ape shit on me."

"Did he do that to your face?"

"Some of it. My mum did the rest when she came home and found out that I'd pissed Richard off again." He rubbed his jaw wincing.

"Do they beat you a lot?"

He looked like a little boy sitting at my kitchen table. Hurt and vulnerable. He nodded in answer to my question. "Only when I deserve it so I'm told."

"Can't you leave home? Get somewhere of your own?"

"Nope. Got a court order, I have to stay with a parent or it's off to jail, or the nut house."

"Where's your real dad?"

"Burning in hell I expect."

I stood up and got a packet of chocolate hob-nobs out of the cupboard. "Here." I gestured with them.

"Thanks." He said taking a handful.

"So what now?"

"I'll just stay out of their way for a few days then everything'll go back to normal, for a while anyway." He paused for a while before changing the subject. "So how are you then Flynn? What have you been up to, you big acid-tripping hippy?" That made him smile anyway.

"Oh you know, the usual. That LSD messed with my head something wicked. For a time there I was worried that I might have killed you. I thought there was a body in the compost heap."

Sid snorted at that. "Yeah, I've had that before. Once thought I'd hung my sister from a lamppost with piano wire."

"Do you have a piano?"

"Where the fuck would I get a piano from? I don't know where I thought I'd got the wire from." He shook his head bemused.

"I won't be doing it again. It lasts too long."

"Must've been 'cause it was your first time."

"Maybe. Anyway, I've got bigger problems; can you get hold of any more diazepam?"

"Probably. I don't know what I did with the last lot, must have lost them when we were tripping. You didn't find them did you?"

"No." I lied. "But can you get any? I'll pay."

"I'll ring my mate and ask. On one condition."

"Name it."

"Can I sleep in your shed tonight?"

Sleep in the shed? Was this what his life had come to? Sleeping in someone's shed? I couldn't have that, it was out of the question.

"I'll do you one better. I'll get you booked in a bed and breakfast for a couple of days."

"For me? Don't be daft. Honestly, I'll be fine in the shed. At least it'll be warm and dry."

"No, I insist. You get me sorted out with some diazepam and I'll pay you for them and get you a room for a few days."

I spent the next hour filling him in on the problem I was having with running out of risperidone and losing the new prescription. Plus, now I had the bloody stupid blood tests to do which I couldn't keep avoiding forever.

Sid commiserated with me. "I don't have any risperidone either. My sister's shit-head boyfriend nicked 'em while I was out the other day. He nicked everything out of the kitchen cupboard, all the pain killers, sleeping tablets, and my anti-depressants. I'm gonna be a right barrel of laughs for the next few weeks."

"Shit. Sorry. If I had any I'd share them with you."

"Cheers Bud. I might have a borrow of some diazepam though when you get some."

"Goes without saying."

He got his phone out of his pocket. "Right I'll text Martin and ask what he can get us."

I didn't know who Martin was so I just nodded while he engaged in several texts with so called Martin, which culminated in Sid saying "He's on his way."

I let Martin in through the back door when he knocked on the kitchen window. He was a scrawny, pasty, ginger haired, scruffy looking fella', in age somewhere between twenty-five and forty-five.

"Alright?" He greeted me as I opened the door.

"Martin?" I asked.

"Yep." He was fiddling nervously with his goatee. "Is Sid here?"

I held the door open and gestured for him to come in.

"Cheers." He went in and greeted Sid.

He was getting various bottles out of his parker and putting them on the kitchen table as I came back in.

"What you got for us then Mart?" Sid was nosing at the labels on the bottles.

I hovered quietly in the background not quite sure what to do about the prescription drug deal that was going on in my kitchen.

Martin was reeling off the list of pills that he had. "I've got diazepam, temazepam, got some Prozac, and this," he said pulling yet another bottle out of his coat. "This is Tramadol."

Sid picked up the Prozac. "Cool."

"So what do you want?"

Sid and I looked at each other for confirmation before I answered. "All of it." Quickly followed by. "Do you take cheques?" Which was followed by laughter.

I took it that was a no.

Once I had raided Linda's underwear drawer where I knew she kept the emergency money, I concluded my first drug deal.

After Martin had departed, Sid and I divvied up our spoils before I dropped him off at the B&B round the corner from me.

Closing the front door firmly behind me, I let out a sigh of relief. I had the house safely back to myself again. I smiled. Trotting off to the kitchen I took two Prozac and two diazepam, and washed them down with a coffee, before floating away the rest of the afternoon on the couch.

Linda came bursting in later that night. "Flynn? Are you okay? I've been ringing you for the last hour. I've been worried sick."

"What?" I couldn't focus on what she was saying very well.

I sat up yawning, missing most of whatever she was jabbering on about.

She was pointing at me and prattling on in an annoying pitch that was making my teeth grate. "So what?" She asked.

"So what, what?" I shouted back at her.

She gave me a look that made me wince. I got the feeling she might suddenly drop her bottom jaw like a snake and strike to devour me. I recoiled with disgust.

The disgust on my face seemed to aggravate her even more. She had that crazy 'other one' look that I had been trying to convince myself was a figment of my imagination for the last few years.

She sank onto all fours and put her head down with her teeth bared at me, she snarled and saliva dropped from her peeled-back lips onto the carpet. I gave an involuntary shudder, afraid to meet her gaze, yet afraid to take my eyes off her. Then, as quick as I could snap my fingers, 'other Linda' was gone. My sweet wife was smiling down at me adoringly. "You look tired Love." She pulled a blanket up over me, tucking me in. "There, you rest while I cook you something nice for tea." She smiled lovingly and wandered off to the kitchen.

My heart was racing with fear and confusion. What the hell? Had I hallucinated again?

My eyes wandered down to the patch of drool still there on the carpet. That didn't vanish as 'other Linda' did.

Chapter Fifteen

I began paying close attention to Linda and her odd behaviour. The patch of drool on the carpet alarmed me. 'Other Linda' had vanished quick as a flash, yet the drool from her bared fangs lay on the cream shag-pile, testament to the scene I had witnessed. When I questioned her about the mark on the carpet later on, she had insisted I had spilt a glass of water there earlier that morning. I did have a glass of water earlier, but I had no recollection of spilling any.

That night as I lay beside her in bed, I found myself watching her in the moonlight. She slept on her back, with her small feet hanging out of the bottom of the covers, bravely facing the night and the fiends that lurk within it. I preferred the foetal position, feet hidden well under the covers away from any opportunist monsters that may appear; ready to bite my toes off.

I could see a faint smile on her lips as she lay there. I leant up on my elbow to have a closer look. "Ugh." I gave an involuntary shudder. That was one malevolent looking expression. But were her teeth normal below those luscious lips, or were they fangs as they had seemed earlier? As much as the thought terrified me, I had to know.

Gingerly I leaned across to her, cursing the bed for squeaking as I moved. With shaking hands I moved my fingers towards her lips. I tentatively rested my left hand little finger against her top lip ready to gently peal it back to reveal the fangs that she had underneath. With my right index finger I moved to peal the bottom lip away, when she woke up and screamed.

She screamed, then I screamed.

"What the hell are you doing?" She demanded while turning her lamp on.

My brain was scrambled and muddled. "I don't know."

"You don't know? You don't know why you had your fingers in my mouth while I was trying to sleep?"

"I don't know."

"Were you asleep?"

"Yes, I must have been." I paused and tried to compose myself. "Sorry Linda."

She glared at me from over her stiff shoulder as she turned over and clicked the light back off. "Go back to sleep."

"Okay, sorry."

I turned over but there was no way on earth I could sleep now. I'd been right, she was crazy. I was sure I saw that maniac look in her eyes briefly when she had turned the light on. Plus, she'd very nearly bitten me. No, I would have to be very careful around her that was for sure.

Once I was sure that she had gone back to sleep, I crept out and went down the stairs. Normally if I couldn't sleep I would take a sleeping pill, but not from now on. I'd need my wits about me in case Linda flipped and attacked. I would have to be on guard *at all times.*

After rummaging through the kitchen drawer I found what I was desperately looking for - the carving knife Linda had confiscated. I liked the weight of it in my hand. It was reassuringly heavy. I ran my finger down the length of the blade and delighted in the droplets of blood that fell from it. It was sharp enough should I feel the need to use it.

I crept back up the stairs to bed, noting Linda's soft snores as I approached the bed. Good. She was asleep. I stood over her with my knife in my hands feeling much calmer then I had for a while. I walked to the end of the bed where her toes where sticking out from under the covers and with my blade I lifted the covers down over her feet hiding them away from the monsters. I didn't want her feet getting cold or nibbled on. I slid the knife underneath my pillow and slept the rest of the night away without incident.

By breakfast time I had normal Linda back. She was sweet and attentive, fussing over me as she made me my breakfast. No mention at all of the psycho who tried to bite me in the night. I thought it best not to mention it in case I set her off again.

I briefly wondered if perhaps she was schizophrenic. If she was, I wondered what giving her the little pink pill would do? Sadly I had none left with which to share, but I did have Prozac. While she went off to call her dad I put two in her coffee along with a diazepam; at least I might get a day off from psycho Linda then.

She came back with a worried look on her face. "He says he's feeling better, but he sounds terrible." She sat down and picked up her coffee cup laced with pharmaceuticals. My eyes were glued to the cup in her hand. She continued talking without drinking. "I'm sure his Nurse was eavesdropping in the background. I bet that's why he sounded so strange. I'll have to go up and see him, it's no good." She put down her untouched coffee cup and picked up her car keys.

"You don't mean you're going there now? Drink your coffee first." I was panicking.

"If I set off now I can be back in time for work. Can you open up for me if I'm running late?" She slid her shoes on as she spoke.

"Yes of course." I sighed.

I'd have to slip some more in her coffee at work later.

I *did* have to open up at work as Linda must've been running late. I just hoped she'd be back before any customers arrived. I don't cope well with other people, especially when I haven't got the delightfully numbing pink pill in my arsenal. Fortunately though, it was very quiet, and so I got on with my normal duties of watering up and dead-heading the flowers.

By the time I finished Linda was just coming in through the main doors. Thank goodness. I walked over to greet her. "How did it go?"

She took off her sunglasses to reveal tearstained puffy eyes. "Not good."

She went through to the office and I heard her put the kettle on as I followed after her.

Shit. No time to slip anything into her coffee. She followed my eyes with hers to the cup she was holding. "What?"

"Nothing. What happened at your dad's?"

"I've got rid of the nurse."

"Why?"

"Because he was an idiot. And I think he might have been bullying my dad a bit. He never came out and said it, but I know something wasn't right. So I sent the idiot packing."

"But what about your dad? Who's gonna take care of him?"

"Me and cousin Josie are gonna do it between us. Plus his next-door neighbour Irene said she'd look in on him for us when we aren't there. It'll be fine, don't worry."

I smiled at her trying not to look worried.

Chapter Sixteen

By midday I had a blinding headache and was getting irritable, so Linda sent me home to calm down for a bit. I thought I'd been masking my oncoming bad temper very well, but apparently not, as Linda had been watching me carefully all morning. She'd 'noticed the warning signs' apparently. I wondered if she'd realised I was onto her?

I had been studying her intently. From the aggressive way she closed the office door behind her, to the irrational way that she would not touch any cup of coffee that I put in front of her. She just wasn't normal.

It didn't matter, I was glad to be away for a while so that I could relax for a bit. I slid behind the steering wheel of my van and headed for home. After having second thoughts, I decided to go see how Sid was getting on at the B&B he was staying at. I had text him a few times but he hadn't replied. On trying to phone him I got told by an operator that 'the mobile I was calling was switched off'. I was getting a little worried about him.

I pulled up outside of the pleasant looking Victorian townhouse and strolled up to the front door. It was locked, so I pressed the bell and waited for someone to come.

"Hello, can I help you?" A little old lady was standing behind me, looking up at me expectantly.

"Yes, sorry, you made me jump." I flustered. "I was just looking for my friend Sid? He booked in yesterday."

She drew her eyebrows together in a not-quite frown. "Sorry, he's gone."

"Gone?"

"Gone. He stayed for about an hour and then left. Without paying I might add."

Mm. I had given Sid the money to pay for his lodgings, perhaps I should have gone in and paid myself. I pulled my wallet out. "How much does he owe?"

She waved it away. "Nothing it's okay, he didn't use anything or make a mess. I rented the room back out again a few hours later, so no harm done. This time." She added.

I put my wallet back in my pocket. "Thank you, sorry for any inconvenience. Did he say where he was going?"

"No, I never saw him go. Sorry."

"Well thank you anyway."

"Good bye."

She went in through the front door leaving me stood on the doorstep, unsure of what to do next.

I got back in my van to think. Where would he go? I knew he wasn't in my shed as I went in there this morning to get a hacksaw blade that would fit behind the toilet cistern in case Linda should try and attack me while I was on the toilet.

The only place I thought I could look for him was where I had picked him up from. 118 High Street. I didn't think he would go back there, but I had to start somewhere.

I arrived at 118 High St. and felt my mood sink. It was a very dreary place indeed. I sat looking at the house for a few minutes wondering if I dare go knock on the door. Sid's parents were obviously violent from what he'd told me. What if they set about me? Shit I wish I'd brought my knife. Note to self, get a weapon that will fit in your pocket!

I glanced in my rear-view mirror and noticed a car parked a few spaces behind me. It stuck out like a sore thumb in amongst the old Fiestas and Peugeots down this street. A big new silver Mercedes. I had a closer look and noted someone sitting in the driver's seat. Were they watching me? I wondered. Why would they be watching me? Were they drug-dealers? Was I on their turf? Oh fuck, I've seen Boyz in the Hood; I know what happens in places like this.

I slid down further in my seat hoping that they hadn't noticed me. Oh god. Now I couldn't see in the rear-view mirror to know what they were doing. Oh Christ I just heard a car door! Oh my god someone's coming to kill me!

I thought that I better get the hell out of there quickly before someone blew my head off. I went to turn the key in the ignition but my hand found nothing. Where's the key? I panicked looking all around me for the key that I must have taken from the ignition.

I was just going through my pockets when I heard a bang on the window. I leaped out of my skin and almost threw-up with fright. I turned to see the horrid gangster who was about to shoot me, but found instead a pretty middle-aged woman. Very well dressed, designer suit, Ivana Trump hair. Definitely not the tracksuit and gold chained thug I had imagined. She knocked on the window again impatiently and gestured for me to wind the window down. I obliged her seeing as I saw no evidence of a gun.

"Sorry." I mouthed to her as I stuck the key in the ignition and started the engine so that my electric window would work. I pressed the button and wound the window down before turning the ignition back off.

She spoke first. "Do you know the resident of this house?"

"Maybe. What do you want with him?" Was she a high-class bailiff? Loan shark?

"He's my son."

Okay not what I expected. She didn't look at all like Sid's description of her.

"Sid is your son?"

"Who?"

"Sid. The boy that lives here."

"You mean Bobby?"

"Bobby? No. Sid."

She put her head in her hands and turned away from me. I don't like seeing women upset, Linda says that makes me sexist, but I disagree, I think it just means I'm a caring cave man. I got out and closed the car door behind me.

She turned towards me obviously distressed. "Do you know about my son's...problems?" She pointed to her head.

I nodded. "Yes. That's how we met. I'm brain-damaged, and we met at the hospital." I suddenly remembered my manners. "I'm Flynn by the way." I held my hand out for her to shake, which she accepted.

"I'm Susan. So you know about my son's *personality disorder*?" She spoke the last part quietly, obviously embarrassed about people hearing her.

"Yes." I looked back at the house. "Have you knocked to see if he's in?" Wait a minute. I was getting confused. "Don't you live there?"

She looked very annoyed as she snapped back. "I do not live there!" She composed herself before continuing. "I knocked but there's no one home. Do you have any idea where Bobby is?"

"I know where he was. Look, we can't stand here all day. Would you like to go and get a cup of coffee while I tell you what I know? There's a nice coffee place just up the road."

This seemed to placate her. "Yes, that would be agreeable."

Chapter Seventeen

I set off towards the coffee shop with Susan following behind me in her car. I pulled into my usual spot in the corner of the little car park at the side of the café. Susan pulled into a space opposite me and after locking up her car, followed me into the little coffee shop.

I loved this place. I breathed in the heavy heady aroma as we went in through the doors. Linda and I came in here all the time. We were both addicted to the cappuccinos that they served here.

I ordered a cappuccino for myself and turned to Susan. "What would you like?"

"Could I have a skinny latte please? Do you mind if I just use the rest room?"

"Not at all. I'll find us a table and fetch the drinks over."

She smiled sadly and left through the door marked ladies'.

"Hello Flynn." A waitress greeted me as she passed. "Here again I see."

"It's your fault for making such good coffee." I countered.

"Are you here alone? Or is Linda hiding somewhere?" She peered behind me smiling.

"No she's busy at work today. I'm here with a friend."

I sat down at my usual table in the corner, as the waitress went off to take someone's order.

Susan returned looking a little puffy around the eyes. I think she must have been crying. I wasn't sure what to do but I was sure it probably wasn't appropriate to pat her on the head as I would do to Linda. I realised I was staring so looked away quickly.

"Thank you for the coffee."

"You're welcome."

She sighed and stirred the cream around her cup. "How long have you known Bobby?"

"Who? Oh Sid? Few weeks maybe. You?"

"All his life. I gave birth to him remember."

"Sorry." I rolled my eyes at my stupidity. "I'm not very good at socialising anymore. Since the head injury."

"That's okay. You're doing very well." She gave me an encouraging smile. She was nice, I liked her.

"I got a text from him yesterday to come and pick him up. When I got to his house, he was black-and-blue and told me that his step-dad had beaten him up for taking his car, then you, I presume, hit him again for upsetting his step-dad."

She looked at me in disbelief. "He really told you all that?"

"Yes. He didn't want to go back home, so I booked him into a B&B around the corner from me. Except he left after an hour, now I don't know where he is and he isn't answering his phone."

"You're obviously a good friend Flynn." She reached across and put her hand over mine. "Thank you for taking care of him. However, I assure you, the version of events my son told you about is wildly incorrect."

I sighed and looked at her. She seemed sincere, so I asked the question that was bugging me. "Why does he call himself Sid?"

She raised her eyebrows and looked as though she was trying to find the right words. "Bobby had a twin brother called Sid. They weren't identical twins, but they were inseparable from the moment they were born. Bobby was the shy reserved one, the one who didn't want to be in trouble. He was the good one if you will. Sid, on the other hand, *the real Sid*, that is, he was the very devil himself. No that's harsh." She corrected herself. "He wasn't a bad boy, just very, very disturbed. If there was trouble to be had, Sid would find it. He was always dragging Bobby off on some wild caper." She paused to have a sip of her coffee. "When the boys were nine, Sid decided to steal the car. He'd been watching me and his father driving for a while until he had convinced himself that he could drive too. He got up in the middle of the night and dragged Bobby out of the house with him. Bobby didn't want to go, but Sid got what Sid wanted. He threatened to drown Bobby's pet rabbit if he didn't go with him. They were lucky that night. They crashed into the rubbish bins at the end of the drive and stalled the car. My husband Patrick heard the crash and went running. Bobby was sat in the passenger side crying with a bloody nose where he had banged it against the windscreen when they crashed. Sid was furious at being caught before he'd had a chance to drive anywhere. He wasn't in the least sorry.

As they both got older, Bobby became more and more introverted and Sid got more and more aggressive. Sid would often get violent with Bobby, hurting him when he wouldn't go along with whatever hair-brain scheme he had planned. By the time Bobby was twelve, he developed an awful nervous stammer. I took him to a speech therapist who implied the stammer was due to over-anxiety stemming from his brother's behaviour. I had enough by that point and sent Sid to a therapist; I wanted some answers about what was going on inside his head. After seeking the advice of several doctors and councillors they came to the conclusion that Sid had a personality disorder coupled with hyper-mania. We tried therapy, anger management, medication, but nothing made any difference. Plus, the worse Sid got, the more Bobby suffered. His stammer became so bad that we had to take him out of school. He was getting bullied relentlessly for it. I had to home-school him for the last few years, while Sid had to go off to a private school that specialised in looking after problem children." She fell into her own thoughts, and drank the last of her coffee.

I hadn't expected any of this when I went to call on 'Sid' this morning. But, she wasn't finished.

"With Sid away at private school, Bobby started to get better. He started to relax a little, even engaging in conversation again. We finally thought that we were making progress, until Sid broke out and came home.

The school alerted us to his breakout as soon as it was discovered that he had left the premises, so we were on alert. Three days later, and still no Sid. We had been sure that he would turn up on our doorstep. He was fourteen, where else could he go? As it happened, he had come straight home, unbeknown to us; he had been living in the shed at the bottom of the garden. Bobby knew, but Sid had told him that if he told on him he would kill his dog. So poor Bobby kept his mouth shut, which is a shame because Sid had already killed the poor thing anyway.

Sid was angry at being sent away, and so the first chance he got, he came back to get his revenge.

The first I knew about any of it was when I got up in the night to go use the bathroom and smelled smoke as I opened the bedroom door. I panicked and flicked the light on to see the landing filled with thick black smoke. I looked up through the dark haze to see the smoke alarm hanging off the ceiling with its battery torn out. I went rushing into the bedroom to wake my husband Patrick before running into Bobby's room to get him up and out of the house."

I interrupted her. "My god how frightening!"

"It was. But worse was to come. My husband, Bobby and I, fought our way down the stairs past the flames and managed to get to the back door. The only problem was, Sid had locked us all in and taken the keys. He was looking at us through the kitchen window dangling the keys at us, laughing.

We banged and banged at the windows desperately trying to break the glass. Sid had even taken all the window lock keys with him, he had planned it all thoroughly, we were completely trapped. It was getting hotter and hotter in there, and the smoke was horrendous. We managed to get wet tea-towels across our mouths trying to keep the choking at bay. We knew we didn't have long. It was Bobby that saved me, and him of course. He realised something me and my husband hadn't - the dog flap in the laundry room door only locked from the inside. It was a tight squeeze, but Bobby and I managed to get through it. My husband didn't.

Once Bobby and I were outside I chased Sid desperately trying to get the keys back off him to let my husband out. The little so-and-so laughed at me and kept running away, dangling the keys, taunting me. He was so busy laughing at my tears and trying to grab the keys that he didn't notice Bobby creeping up behind him with the baseball bat that he had been playing with earlier. Bobby hit Sid so hard that he broke his neck and died instantly. Bobby grabbed the keys as I dropped to my knees in shock and ran over to let his father out." She stopped while she got her voice back under control.

"It was too late. He was dead. I don't know what sight Bobby saw when he opened that kitchen door but it traumatised him so much he didn't speak for over a year. He's been in and out of mental institutions ever since."

I sat back in my chair stunned. I looked down into my cold cup of coffee, unsure how to respond.

She asked me. "So now he wishes to be called Sid? I find that very disturbing."

"That's who he introduced himself as." I paused. "Is he dangerous?"

She flicked her gaze up to mine. "No. Just, damaged."

"Whose house is it that he lives at? He said he lived there with you and a step-dad called Richard, and that you both beat him. I've seen the bruises."

"That's Bobby's house or Sid as you know him. The rents cheap and it's near local amenities. Myself or his step-dad Richard stop by frequently to make sure he's okay. He's seemed better for having a little independence. He is twenty-four now after all."

"I thought he was lying about his age. He looks so young."

"He's always had a baby face."

"So what about the bruises I saw yesterday?"

"What he told you is half-true. He did steal Richard's car, but not to joy ride in." She paused trying to regain her composure. "He ran a hose pipe from the exhaust pipe and in through the driver-side window. He tried to kill himself. The bruises are from him passing out and hitting his head on the steering wheel. Some of them anyway, the rest came from the paramedics when they revived him."

I was stunned. "Poor Sid. He seemed fine before. Well apart from his sister's boyfriend stealing his medication."

"He doesn't have a sister."

My head was starting to ache.

She patted my hand again. "Now you know why I need to find him."

We parted after exchanging numbers and promising to keep in touch if either of us saw Bobby/Sid.

Chapter Eighteen

My head was reeling from it all. I thought I had problems!

To think I was going to ask Sid if he thought Linda was crazy. How would he know!

Which one of him would I ask?

I went home to think about things.

I was a little disturbed to see that my supply of Prozac was dwindling, probably because I'd tried to drug Linda such a lot. I'd better be careful now and try and make it last until next week. It wasn't like I could ask Sid to get some more now could I.

Good god I was the only sane person in my life wasn't I?

I was just getting ready to go up to bed for a cat nap when I received a text from Susan.

Thank you for today
love Susan xxx

I smiled. She was a nice woman, which is surprising with all that she had been through. I text her straight back.

Any time, I can always meet you if
you need me xx

I then went upstairs and got into bed to sleep the rest of my headache and the day away.

I awoke with a start at the bang I heard downstairs. I shot up and grabbed my knife from under the pillow, pulled my clothes on and headed cautiously down the stairs. It must be burglars. The bang I heard must've been them kicking the door in. Never mind, this time I was armed.

I crept down the hallway towards the kitchen -still hearing the sound of doors slamming and drawers banging. My god they were ransacking the house! I took a deep breath and tried to get my shaking hands under control. "I can do this." I told myself under my breath. I had the knife in my right hand. leaving me to negotiate the door handle with my damaged left hand which was no easy feat on the best of days. I was just fumbling with it trying to get it open when a voice bellowed making me fall back with fright.

"Flynn? Is that you?" It was Linda. Oh my god the relief. And anger. How could she *scare* me like that? She's supposed to be my carer; she's supposed to be considerate to my needs *-and nerves*. I slid the knife up my sleeve so that she wouldn't see it as she flung the door open.

"What are you doing?" She looked puzzled at me.

"What the hell do you think you were doing making all that racket? You scared the shit out of me you stupid cow." I was getting really angry now.

"I was putting the shopping away. I'm sorry if I made too much noise, I was going as quiet as I could." Her lip started to wobble.

"Oh don't come the theatrics with me. You know very well you're in the wrong." I pointed at her with my stumps. "You're doing it on purpose aren't you? Trying to wind me up. Well if you want a fight you can fucking have one." I pushed her with my left hand.

I saw something flash across her eyes that made me shudder despite my anger. I saw a quiet calculated rage peer out at me. Before I had chance to recoil she struck out with her fist and hit me full pelt in the temple. I went down with a bang into darkness.

I slowly opened my eyes wincing at the pin prick of light that seemed to be coming towards me, getting larger and larger, blinding me with its brightness. I started to become aware of voices around me. "Mr Locke? Can you hear me Mr Locke?"

"Flynn? It's Linda. Open your eyes."

Then the other voice again. "We'll have to get him an ambulance."

I blinked and my vision started to clear.

"Mr Locke? Flynn?"

"Yes." I tried to sit up but found I was trapped. I started to panic, fighting against my restraints.

"It's okay Flynn." It was Linda looking down at me crying. "It's your seat belt that's holding you still. Here I'll undo it." She leant across me and undid the seatbelt.

"What the hell is going on? I was in my hallway a moment ago?"

I was interrupted by a paramedic shining a torch into my eyes. I cringed and tried to look away but he held my head still with his other hand. "Please stay still a moment."

Linda looked in shock. "I just got home from work and found you here."

I looked around me to find that I was in my van - which was halfway through the shed at the bottom of my garden. I must have blacked out on my way in through the drive and crashed through the shed at the bottom. "My head hurts." I told the paramedic.

"We're going to take you into hospital; I want to make sure that you don't have a concussion. It looks like you hit your head hard."

I blinked my confusion at him. "I don't understand."

I was loaded up into an ambulance and taken to the infirmary. Linda was sitting opposite me in the ambulance with her arm outreached in order to hold my hand. She looked at me with worry etched onto her face. I eyed her nervously.

Had she hit me?

Had I blacked out and hallucinated again? I looked closer at her. She wasn't even wearing the same clothes as she had in my version of events earlier. When she hit me she had been wearing a green blouse. Now she was wearing a light blue shirt. I screwed my eyes up in frustration. How can I trust anything that my brain tells me? Dr Patel had told me that if I came off the Risperidone too fast that my perception would go haywire and I could potentially hallucinate. I'd gone and done it now hadn't I? Obviously the Prozac and diazepam weren't working like I had thought they were. I sighed.

"It's okay Love; we'll be there in a minute." She squeezed my hand. "You scared the life out of me when I found you like that."

I sat up a little. "So I never went inside the house?"

"I don't think so."

"So we never had a fight?"

She looked distressed. "You aren't having hallucinations again are you? I promise, we haven't had a fight. The last I saw of you was when you left work earlier."

I shook my head and felt tears slide down my face. "I don't want to be like this." The sob broke free and I wept.

I was settled into a private room -what with me being a nutcase I presume. The nurses must have read my medical records as they seemed very nervous around me. Maybe I give off the 'nutter' vibe these days? I was given painkillers which helped enormously. I gingerly touched the sore spot on my temple. I must have cracked it on the steering wheel.

Linda went off to find a coffee machine giving me a little while to gather my thoughts.

Did I go and see Susan at the café? Is there a Susan or did my fried brain invent her? One way to check, I thought. I could feel my mobile phone sticking into my ribs from my pocket. I slid it out and checked my texts. I distinctively remembered her texting me and me texting her back, from home. I flipped through my texts finding nothing from Susan at all. The last text I had received had been from Sid the previous day. "Shit!" I exclaimed. Was none of it real? I flipped through my phone book, and to my immense relief, found Susan's number.

She was real. We had met in the café, and we had exchanged numbers. Phew. The relief was immense. So had I invented the rest then? I must have driven home from the café and blacked out in the driveway and dreamed the rest. And I always maintain I don't dream?

"Ah now Mr Locke." The young doctor announced as he flung my curtain back. "You look much brighter than earlier. I don't see any signs of a concussion, just a few bruises, so I don't see any reason why you can't go home soon." He looked down at my notes. "But I see from your medical records that there is an outstanding request for some blood tests. A nurse will be along in a moment to take some blood from you and to give you something for the pain to take home with you." Then he was gone.

Linda had just entered the room in time to hear about my impending blood tests. I was hoping she wouldn't hear so that I could scarper before they tried to take my blood and my lies would be exposed. But no. There was no getting away from it this time. Linda wouldn't hear my protests for not wanting to waste any more time in hospital when I'll be back there on Thursday anyway. "You're having them." She said with a no-nonsense tone in her voice.

I sat back on the bed scowling.

"While we're alone." She dropped her voice to a whisper. "What was all that blood in the back of your van?"

My heart sank and I started to feel faint. "What blood?"

"There's blood splatters all over the back of your van. I thought it was yours when I found you but you don't have any cuts on you anywhere. So where did it come from?"

"I don't know."

She didn't question me anymore as the nurse came in to take my blood. She was an unsmiling bitch that seems to take great pleasure in stabbing me with her needle. Once I had a bit of cotton wool and a plaster over my wound, I grabbed my little bag of pain killers we got a taxi and went home.

Linda was very quiet all the way home. I think she was frightened of me.

On arriving back I was sent up to bed. Linda said she'd bring me a cup of tea and a pain killer once I had gotten settled in bed. I pulled the covers up over my chin and got comfortable. I thought I had already been to bed once that day, but apparently not. None of it had happened. I hadn't heard what I thought was a burglar banging about downstairs. I hadn't pulled my knife out from under my pillow....................Wait a minute! My Knife! If none of it happened, my knife would still be under my pillow where I left it.

I sat up and pulled my pillows away from the bed. The knife was gone.

Chapter Nineteen

I opened my eyes to find myself back on the number 30 bus. I was back on the top deck at the front again. I leant forward to look down through the window that showed the driver below. 'Other me' winked at me from the driver's seat below, causing me to sit back in my seat with alarm.

"I know it's a dream, I know it's a dream, I know it's a dream." I chanted rocking back and forth with my eyes shut. I opened my eyes as I heard shuffling footsteps behind me. I shot round to view the bus's new passengers. I noted the two mutilated women from the last bus trip, along with a young man who looked vaguely familiar. He came down the aisle towards me and settled into the seat behind me, resting his backpack on the seat beside him. He nodded to me as if he recognised me too. The two women disappeared towards the back of the bus to my great relief.

I turned back to look at the strange man. Who was he? He just stared back at me with a fixed smile on his face. There was something very sinister about him, despite the smile.

"Do I know you?" My voice wavered.

Before my companion had time to reply to my question we were interrupted by the driver's tannoy. 'Other me's' voice came bellowing out of the speaker above me. "Last stop Marble Arch. Next stop Daynejonne. This bus will self-destruct in 10, 9, 8…."

"No!" I cried. I realised who the man was as he picked up his backpack grinning at me.

"7, 6, 5…"

"No please no. Not again."

The women from the back started laughing hysterically.

"4, 3, 2…"

The man behind me winked at me as he pressed the button.

"1."

The white heat swept through the top deck like a tidal wave of fire. I felt my flesh vaporize and my eyeballs implode. I tried to scream but the sound came out gargled through melted tissue that was once my throat.

I woke up screaming with Linda rocking me back and forwards.

"Please don't let it be real!" I cried with tears cascading down my cheeks. I sniffed through my hysterical sobs. "I don't want to remember."

Linda was crying too, holding me tight in her arms, trying to stop me shaking. "It's okay," she told me. "I've got you. I've got you."

Once my panic subsided a little I was devastated to find that I had wet the bed. I was so embarrassed. I hadn't wet the bed since I was little.

Linda ran me a bath while she pulled the soaking sheets off the bed and changed them for fresh linen.

"Linda, I'm so sorry." I told her as she came into the bathroom to check on me.

"It's fine." She knelt down beside me and rested her head against my wet arm that was hanging over the side of the tub. "I hate that you have all these awful memories hanging about in your head, torturing you."

I sighed a deep sigh. "It was hell on earth on that bus. I don't want to remember it. I'm just glad you never saw any of it."

"I have a vivid imagination. I saw enough from the wreckage afterwards to make a good guess."

I looked away. She thought she knew, but she really, really didn't.

She looked back up at me suddenly. "Would hypnotism help do you think?"

"What do you mean? I don't want to remember, I remember too much."

"No I don't mean that. I mean to make you forget."

It wasn't anything that had really occurred to me before. "I'll give it some thought."

She gave me a sad smile and after kissing me tenderly on the lips, left me to my thoughts. Twenty minutes later and I was back in bed, lying upon fresh linen beside my wife who loved me.

The following day I felt much better. I got up, got dressed, and took my Prozac/Diazepam cocktail. It was good to be back in a routine again.

Linda had reversed my van back out from the shed and had spent hours cleaning the back of it out. There wasn't much damage to the van, just a few scratches here and there. The shed would have to be demolished though, that was beyond repair. I was just looking out through the kitchen window when Linda came in carrying my carving knife.

"I found this in the driver's door pocket." She looked very pale and worried. I could virtually smell the fear coming off her. She set the knife down on the kitchen table. "What were you doing with it?"

Good god what could I say? Not that I was keeping it to defend myself from her! God think brain! "I don't remember taking it from the house." I said truthfully.

She pursed her lips and dropped it into the dishwasher tray before setting it onto 'sanitize wash'. She stood at the sink for a while with her back to me. I could see the tension built up in her shoulders. "I'll just go hang the washing out before I go." She said robotically.

It had been decided that I would take the day off to recuperate after my 'episode' yesterday. Plus, I think Linda was nervous about me driving if I was having blackouts again. To be honest, Linda seemed nervous around me full stop. Another problem was, Linda would have to go straight from work to her dad's house, as today was her day for looking after him. She had rung her cousin in the morning desperately trying to get her to swap days with her, but Josie said it wasn't possible. She was worried about me being on my own for too long, but to be honest, I was looking forward to it. I couldn't keep up the numb act twenty-four hours a day, it was too draining. Plus I didn't have enough tablets left to dose myself properly into a sufficiently numb state.

In the end she went, all be it reluctantly. I heaved a sigh of relief as she went.

I made myself busy tearing down the rest of the shed. At least it was something useful that I could get on with. I was halfway through when my phone started beeping. I pulled it out of my pocket to see who was texting me.

R U busy? Can I come round?
Sid

So he wasn't hiding from me then. I wanted to know what the hell had been going on, so I text him back.

Come on round,
I'm at home, got day off

It can't have been more than ten minutes before he found me in the garden taking the last of the shed walls down. He arrived just in time to help me lower the last side down to the floor before I could drop it.

"Spot on timing Sid." I had to really concentrate on not calling him Bobby.

"Glad to help." He said without smiling. "Can we go inside and talk? I think I've done something really bad."

He did look rough. His bruises had yellowed off a lot, but he had huge black bags underneath his dark eyes. He also looked like he needed a good bath.

I gestured for him to follow me inside.

I put the kettle on as I couldn't think of how to start a conversation with him. I knew too much now, or maybe not enough? Fortunately Sid broke the awkward silence for me.

He sat down at the table with a sigh. "So I hear you've been talking to my mum?"

I turned to face him. "Yes. I bumped into her when I went back to your house looking for you. So she found you then."

"Obviously."

I went back to making the tea, unsure of how to proceed with him.

He seemed to sense my wariness and carried on. "Well at least now you know all about my 'trauma'." He did the air quotes.

"I'm sorry." I paused while I gathered my thoughts. "I really didn't mean to pry. It's just that your mum was worried about you and I think she just needed someone to talk to."

Sid put his head in his hands and peered out at me through his fingers. "I think I've done something really bad."

I moved to the chair next to him and slid his cup of tea over to him. "It's okay, you can tell me. I won't tell anyone else."

He looked up at me with moist eyes. "Do you promise you won't say anything to anyone? I mean it, ANYONE?"

"Promise." I was getting unnerved now.

"After I tried to….you know…..myself in Richard's car, they decided to have me committed again. What the hell did they think that'd do to me? Look at Sid, he looks miserable, let's lock him up on a mental ward see how that cheers him up! I don't think so! So I legged it. That's why I wanted to get away from the house; I knew they'd look for me there."

"So why didn't you stay at the B&B?"

He raised his eyebrows in disbelief. "The woman in the room next door to me used to be my mum's cleaner. She knew me! I had to get out of there quick before she grassed me up."

"So then where did you go?"

He took a deep breath, slowly exhaling. "I went back home and hid."

"So you were there when I was outside your door?"

"Yeah. Same with my Mum."

I was puzzled about something Susan had said. "Your mum said you haven't got a sister? So do you live alone? Why did you say you had a sister?"

"She's not technically my sister, no. But we've known each other our whole lives. She's *like* my sister. I do live with her, I have one bedroom, she has the other, but she's gone on a drugs run with the shit-head boyfriend. She's not back till tomorrow."

Nothing and everything all made sense to me at the same time. Plus my head was starting to hurt.

Sid turned to face me. "I need to ask you something VERY important."

"Okay."

"I know you went for a coffee with my mum."

"Yes."

"Then you text her later on and asked to meet her."

"What? No."

"You didn't meet up with her? Do you mean she didn't show up?" Sid was starting to shake a little and his breathing was getting shallow. He looked on the verge of a full-blown panic attack to me.

"I didn't text her, didn't meet up with her."

"You're joking me?"

"Why would I?"

"Why would you?" He said softly to himself.

"Sid? What the hell's going on?"

He stood up and started pacing around the kitchen, taking panicky jerky strides back and forth.

"A few hours after you and Mum left the coffee house, she came back to my house for one last try. I hadn't been expecting her to come back after she left earlier, so I dropped acid. I thought it might make me feel better, and pass the time a bit. She said she had a look around under all the rocks and stuff in the garden and found a spare door key that Bonny - my sort of sister, had left for emergencies. So she let herself in."

I nodded waiting for him to continue.

"She seemed really relieved to see me at first. Gave me a big hug and stuff. Told me all about meeting up with you, and the stuff that you talked about." He paused. "But then after that everything kind of got hazy as the acid kicked in. I'm sure we had a row; then I think her phone went and it was you texting her wanting to meet up or something; and then I think we had a big fight."

"She won't hold an argument against you Sid. She loves you, she'll be back."

He shook his head. "You don't understand. She's missing."

"Missing?" I felt my stomach drop.

He nodded. "Flynn? I think I might have killed her while I was out of it."

Chapter Twenty

"What on earth makes you think that?"

"Richard's been leaving messages for me all night trying to find her. Then the police found her car dumped this morning…" He paused to get his voice back under control. "They found her blood in the car."

I put my hand across my mouth in shock. "Oh my god! I'm so sorry." I felt sick. I shook my head at him.

"What if I did it though? I was that off my tits I could have done it and not remember!"

"You wouldn't."

"But what if I did? I was sure that you text her to meet up with her, but you say that never happened. What the hell else has or hasn't happened?"

I pulled my phone out of my pocket and scrolled through my messages, both sent and received. I passed it over to Sid. "Look, the only person who's text me or who I've text is you."

He looked up and nodded. "I just don't know what to do."

"Are you going to the police? They'll probably want to talk to both of us, we're probably both suspects."

"Fuck that, they'll lock me up in a nut house and throw away the key."

"What about me? Should I hand myself in?"

"They'd do the same to you. So no."

We sat in silence for a while each with our own thoughts.

"I'm really sorry about your mum. She was a lovely lady. I liked her a real lot."

That burst the dam in Sid and he wept like a child while I held him and rocked him as Linda did to me so often.

He stayed with me for most of the day. Linda wouldn't be back until very late, so at least Sid had company. He had become quite subdued now that he had gotten his fears off his chest. We watched the news together in silence, as we saw the footage of Susan's Mercedes being carted off by forensics.

I cooked us dinner and sent Sid off to get a bath while I dug out some old clothes of mine for him to wear. Once he was clean and fed he did look a bit brighter.

"Can I ask you something?" I questioned him.

"Um." He nodded.

"Why do you call yourself Sid?"

He looked down as if trying to find the words. "Bobby was a victim. He was pathetic and weak. He hated himself. Sid however, is strong, tough, take-no-shit. Sid thinks Fuck em all!"

"Okay."

"When I was given the pink pill as you call it, it was supposed to stop my so called multiple personality disorder, which it did. Except Bobby left with the others, and me, Sid, remained."

This poor kid was bat shit crazy. He was way madder than me. "So what happens now you've run out of the pink pill too?"

"Guess we'll have to wait and see."

I got him booked in at a different B&B where hopefully he would go undetected. Plus I paid the receptionist directly this time. I also made sure to book him under a different name. I didn't want the police finding him and locking him up, because if they did, I was sure they would be very interested to talk to me. And after all I had a van covered in blood from that night that I had the blackout. I didn't believe that either Sid or myself had anything to do with Susan's disappearance, I think it's all just a dreadful coincidence, but it's how things could look isn't it?

I went to bed early before Linda came home. I pretended to be asleep when she came in, as I didn't trust myself to look her in the eye and not blab that there was a possibility that either I was a murderer, or, my schizo friend - who she'd never heard of was a murderer.

Both Sid and I kept our heads down for the next few days. We text back and forth as we watched the developments on the news, but that was all. There had been no more new leads with Susan. No body had been found yet, and there were no suspects as yet. Police had appealed for her son to come forward for questioning though.

"Good luck with that." Sid had said.

I went into work with Linda on the Tuesday. She had deemed me safe to be around again I think. I had been pretty subdued for days, but it wasn't due to the pink pill as she thought, it was due to the shock of possibly being implicated in a murder. Before all this I had never even had a speeding fine. Now look at me? Look at what life without the pink pill had turned out to be like! I couldn't wait to be numb again.

I hated feeling these things all of the time. The novelty of emotion has definitely worn off now. I just had today and Wednesday to get through, and then I could go see Dr Patel and get the medication I was supposed to be taking. Then hopefully when the new tablets kicked in, all of this would just be a bad dream.

Linda seemed a little odd with me in the car when we set off for work. We were listening to the radio when the bloody song that haunts my dreams came on the stereo. The DJ announced, "Next up, *Never tear us apart*, by *INXS*."

Before the first notes got played, Linda shot out her hand and turned it off quick. I looked at her questioningly. Did she know that I always had that song in my head? I had never mentioned it.

"You used to love that song." I observed.

"Yeah well now I'm sick of it. It sticks in my head something wicked."

"I know what you mean there." I nodded my agreement.

"What do you mean?" She snapped her head round at me sharply.

Whoa she looked mean. "I just mean it sticks in my head too. That's all."

"Mm." She glared at me and turned back to face forward.

Ouch, someone was in a strange mood. I hope 'other Linda' wasn't coming out to play again. I had quite enough of people and their 'other's' to last me a life time.

I watched her carefully all day at work. She was definitely acting strange. I was finding it very difficult to read her expressions. Her lips seemed to be saying one thing, while her expression was saying something else. For example, she told me that I had done a really good job that day coping with my tasks and with the few people that had pestered at me for various things. Yet, her eyes seemed to be saying 'I hate you, and you're useless, why don't you just die.' It was very confusing. Was it just me?

The sooner I got my medication back the better. It would help if I could talk to someone about my predicament, but who could I ask? The only people I knew these days were disturbed. I could have talked to Susan about Linda if she wasn't dead. It was quite an inconvenience.

Perhaps I could talk to Sid when he's in a more normal mood. Then again, he would probably want to meet her to get an idea of what she's like, and I don't think she'd like that one bit.

It was the following evening when I had my brainwave. I needed someone to witness Linda's strange behaviour - preferably without her knowing, but how?

After a while the solution danced into by brain. I almost laughed. The answer was staring me in the face. I would secretly film her.

I was awake all night plotting and planning how best to do it discretely. I was stuck. What if she found the camera? She would definitely know that I was on to her then. If she knew I was onto her would she try to harm me? To shut me up once and for all?

I decided that after my hospital appointment tomorrow I would go and find Sid and ask for his help. Young people were more technologically minded weren't they? He might know of something suitable. Some James Bond spy gadget or something. If I caught Linda acting odd on camera I could play it back a few times to try and gauge if what I was seeing was real or not. Then I could run it by Sid for his opinion. Yes that was a plan I thought. Now just the dreaded hospital appointment to get through tomorrow.

I eventually fell into a troubled sleep.

The following day I found myself back in the tedious waiting room at the hospital. I sat in my usual spot quietly cringing at the chaos that was going on all around me. Thirty minutes after my appointment was supposed to have started the nurses decided that I had to be weighed again.

"Why?" I asked with annoyance.

"It's procedure." The hard-faced bitch told me.

"Procedure to waste my fucking time? That's about right."

"Hey!" She pointed at me. "There's no need for language like that. Any more of that and you'll be asked to leave."

"Good!" I kicked the chair as I went passed and set off on my own to the weighing room. I got myself settled on the scales and waited for another nurse. Hard-faced bitch seemed to have pissed off.

To my surprise it was Dr Patel that came in to weigh me.

"I hear you aren't very happy today Flynn."

"I'm sorry. I shouldn't have snapped at her. It was just the tone of her voice set me off."

"Well let me get you weighed and we'll go and have a chat in my office."

I felt much calmer by the time we got to his office.

"Please sit." He gestured to the seat next to his desk.

I obliged with a sigh waiting for the bollocking that I knew was coming. He didn't say anything; he just stared at me with his hands clasped in his lap.

I couldn't stand the silence any further so I broke it. "I'm sorry I lost my temper with the nurse."

He nodded at me. "I think I understand why you lost your temper Flynn." He glanced down at the papers on his desk. "I have here the results of your blood tests." He sat back with his hands in a steeple looking at me expectantly.

My heart sank as I looked down at my feet with shame flaming on my face.

He looked closely at my guilty expression. "I see by your blood tests that there is no trace of Citalopram in your system. Also, there seems to be a very negligible level of Risperidone. Not anywhere near the amount that should be in your system. However, all this pales into insignificance compared to the large dose of Lysergic acid diethylamide - LSD to you."

"Sorry." I mumbled staring down at the carpet.

He leaned towards me and said kindly. "Come on, talk to me Flynn. I won't judge you, but I need to know what's going on."

I looked up at his sincere expression. I think I can trust him a little bit. "I lost my prescription. I was too afraid to tell you or Linda that I had lost it. So I made do with some Prozac and diazepam that my friend gave me."

"Plus the LSD?"

"He said it would help."

"LSD is entirely unsuitable for someone in your situation. Although recent studies have deduced that it isn't as harmful as once thought, it is extremely detrimental to someone with the symptoms that you suffer from. I understand that you sometimes have problems with perception and delusions, LSD will exacerbate these problems tremendously. Promise me Flynn, no more LSD!"

"I promise doctor. I didn't mean for things to get so out of hand."

"Everybody makes mistakes, even the best of us. I'm going to put you on a different dose than I intended in light of the circumstances. How have you felt for the last week? I suspect you have probably been having mood swings again. Is that the case?"

I nodded.

"Any delusions or hallucinations?"

I took a deep breath and composed myself. "I've had doubts about Linda being a psycho again." I paused. "In fact I was even planning on filming her to prove that she's psychotic. Does that count?"

"Yes it does. You and your wife mentioned previously that you have often had thoughts that she might be out to harm you, before you had the Risperidone. This is happening again?"

"Yes." It was a relief to talk about it. "Most of the time she seems great, really attentive and loving, but then sometimes it seems as though she turns into a demon. It's just the way she looks at me, as though she's possessed or something, and then before I've had chance to register it, the look's gone and she's back to normal like nothing happened."

"And has this only started bothering you again since stopping your medication?"

I nodded.

He shook his head at me. "Your perception isn't working properly Flynn. It's a wonder you haven't done yourself any harm, or others for that matter."

That made me gulp.

He continued. "Any blackouts?"

"No." I lied. I couldn't tell the truth about that or my driving license would be taken away from me.

"Does Linda know of all this?"

"Nothing. I didn't dare tell her in case she lost her temper and hurt me."

He shook his head at me. "I know it's difficult for you to get your head around while your medication isn't working, but try thinking outside the box, thinking with no emotions. Why would Linda harm you? She has looked after you and cared for you throughout everything that you have been through. I've read through your notes extensively. Linda's saved you from overdoses, stemmed the bleeding when you've slit your wrists and got you to the hospital. She intervened and stopped you from jumping off the hospital roof. Ask yourself Flynn; would a woman who wanted you dead prevent you from killing yourself?"

"I suppose it doesn't make sense does it?" I rested my head against my hand. "How many other women would have stuck it out with me this long? I have put her through hell."

"I promise once the new medication kicks in, in a week or so you should start to feel a little more balanced again."

"I hope so doctor, I can't live like this. When you can't trust your own eyes and ears the world is terrifying."

"Here's the new prescription." He handed me the printout. "Go take it to the dispensary on your way out and start it immediately. The dosage will be written on the packet. Now, I want to see you again one week from today. In the meantime if you feel like you're going downhill, please ring my secretary and she'll arrange an emergency appointment with either myself or one of my colleagues."

He shook my hand and dismissed me.

Chapter Twenty-One

Okay so Linda isn't a psycho. It's me. It's always been me. I should have known.

I made sure to take my new pills as soon as I got them. I didn't even wait to get home; I bought a drink on the way and took the pills in the car. I couldn't wait to get back to normal. At least I knew now that I couldn't trust my own judgement. From now on Linda was the boss.

It had helped a lot talking to Dr Patel, plus he hadn't gone mad about the LSD like I thought he would've. He'd been quite good about it really. And I meant to keep my promise, definitely no more LSD. Reality was fucked up enough without making it worse.

I arrived home to find the phone screaming out at me before I could barely get through the front door. I shot over to it as fast as I could but the bastard thing stopped just as I got there. "SHIT!" I shouted at it. I went back to close the front door properly and dropped my keys on the hall table before going back to the phone to dial 1471. It was a number I didn't recognise so I just pressed 3 to return the call.

After a few rings someone answered. "Hello?"

"Hello someone just called me from this number but I didn't get to the phone in time."

"Flynn?"

"Yes. Who is it?"

"A friend."

My stomach fluttered and dropped a little. "Which friend?"

"It doesn't matter. Listen carefully. Are you listening?"

"Yes."

"You have to go and see Linda's father. Trust me. You have to go see him."

"Why me? Linda takes care of him."

Click. The phone went dead.

I stood there for a few moments with the receiver still in my hand trying to take in what the hell had just happened. I put the receiver back in the cradle and went off to have a sit down on the couch while I thought about what I had been told. Who the hell was it? It sounded like a woman, but I wasn't sure, the voice was rather husky. What did 'they' mean go see Linda's father? Why? Why call me and say that, if there was a problem, why not call Linda? Plus, why wouldn't they give their name?

Yes it was a real head scratcher.

Shortly after, the phone went again. It was Linda.

"Hey, it's me. How did you get on today?"

"Oh fine. Nothing I couldn't cope with."

"Did you tell Dr Patel about your blackouts?"

"No. But I did tell him I've been a bit off. He's trying me on some new medication to see if that balances me out a bit more."

"Oh god I hate it when they mess about with your medication. Why couldn't they leave it alone?"

"I've been on it too long now he said." I crossed my fingers behind my back as I lied. "It loses its affect after a while."

"I suppose that does explain why you've had blackouts again." She sounded doubtful though.

"He says this new stuff will be a lot better once it gets into my system."

"Oh well, worth a try I suppose. Anyway I better go; I've got a customer coming. I'll see you when I get back from my dad's."

"Oh on that subject….."

"Sorry Flynn, I've got to go, I'll see you later. Bye."

"Bye." I said to the dial tone.

Sitting back down huffing at being cut off, I peered over at the note pad next to the telephone. I hadn't realised that I had been doodling on the pad while I had been speaking. Lots of little pictures of squares, crosses and flowers and some gibberish writing that looked like it said 'Daynejonne'. I wondered what that meant. It sounded vaguely familiar.

So I hadn't had chance to tell Linda about the strange phone call I had received. Never mind, I'd tell her later.

I decided to text Sid on the new phone number that I had got for him. We had decided to get him a cheap pay-as-you-go phone from the supermarket, one that couldn't be traced back to him, and more importantly had a new number that only I knew. That way it would make it more difficult for the police to trace him. I pulled my phone out and typed my message.

**Sid, do u wanna get some
fresh air?**

He text straight back.

**R U asking me on a date?
I don't come cheap lol.**

Cheeky sod. I thought.

**Fuck off. lol.
How does cup a tea and fish n chips sound?**

I had a wicked craving for fish and chips.

Gr8 I'm starving.

I picked up my car keys and wallet and set off to pick him up.

"Alright?" He addressed me getting in the passenger side of my van.

"Yeah, you?"

"Fair to middling. Wish I could go home, but, you know, don't want to get locked up in a nut house again."

"Fair enough. Do you fancy going to the seaside for fish n chips? It's always better by the sea than the crap you get around here." I started pulling away from the curb.

"God yeah. I love the seaside." He grinned. "It'll make a nice change."

"Good." I grinned back. "I think a change of scene will do us both good. Do you want to put some music on? There's a load of cd's in the glove box."

"Cool." He started rummaging through my collection tutting with disgust at my musical taste.

"Ah this'll do." He proclaimed holding up my *AC/DC* album *Highway to Hell.*

"Good choice."

We sang our little tone deaf hearts out all the way to the coast and made rude gestures at passing motorists that tutted at us with annoyance. Sid did a spectacular job at hanging his arse out of the window at a coach full of pensioners. Though it was quite embarrassing when half a mile down the road we pulled up level with them at the traffic lights. We both tried to look the other way so as not to make eye contact. But that went out of the window when an old lady got her own back on us by flashing her humongous brassiere at us through the window. That made us laugh, but the rest of the old dears on this bus seemed really annoyed with her. It's nice to see you're never too old to rebel and piss people off.

"I hope I live to be that age." Sid laughed as we pulled back in front of the coach. "If I do, I'm gonna pretend to be deaf, senile, and incontinent just to piss everyone off."

"Yeah, and get one of them mobility scooters so you can terrorise everyone on it."

"That'd be wicked." He laughed. "And I'll get a bumper sticker for it, 'born to be riled!'

I laughed. "I swear half of 'em aren't as senile as they pretend to be. I think it's some private joke at everyone else's expense."

"Yeah how funny would it be to wind up some snot nosed little grandkid by calling em by the wrong name constantly. And think of the drugs you'd get. Have you seen old people's medicine cabinets? They have the lot. My Nana's kitchen cupboard was like a pharmacy."

I laughed and turned the car towards the sea front.

We joined the queue outside of the first chip shop that we came to on the sea front. It was the perfect afternoon to be beside the sea. The sun was high up in the sky, surrounded by thousands of seagulls calling out for scraps from the tourists. Mouth-watering smells of chips and candy-floss floated all around us.

"I love that smell." Sid observed breathing it in deep.

I smiled and turned to the counter to be served.

Leaving the shop armed with a tray of fish and chips each we looked for somewhere to sit.

"Let's go sit on the beach." I decided, leading the way down the stone steps that lead to the sand below.

We bypassed all of the screaming kids and walked further down the beach towards a big pile of rocks.

"This'll do." Sid hopped up on a rock after wiping sand off it.

I perched next to him, facing towards the muddy brown sea.

"This is the life Flynn. Sitting on the beach on a sunny day eating fish n chips." He shovelled a big pile of chips into his mouth.

"Couldn't agree more. I used to come here all the time when I was a kid."

We ate in companionable silence. Once we were full, we laid back to against the rocks to watch the world go by. I decided to approach the subject of Susan.

"Any more news about your mum?"

He shook his head. "Na, but Richard's stopped leaving messages on my old phone now. I only know now what I see on the news."

"I'm sorry."

He rubbed his weary eyes with his hand. "I wonder if I dare go to the funeral."

"But they haven't found a body though have they? There's always hope."

"She's dead. I know she is. I just hope to god it wasn't me that killed her."

I hoped to god it was him that had killed her. But I kept that to myself.

He cleared his throat and changed the subject. "How did it go at the quacks today?"

"Alright really. I shit myself though when he pulled out my blood test results."

"You didn't let them blood test you? I thought you was gonna get out of it?"

"I tried but the bastards practically pinned me down and stole it."

"Shit. What did the doc say?"

"It was pretty much along the lines of 'what the hell have you been doing taking LSD?'"

That made him snort. "What did you say?"

"I had to promise that I wouldn't do it again."

"God what are you, five?"

"I know!"

"Speaking of drugs, I've got some great Skunk if you want to share a joint."

"God I haven't had dope in twenty-odd years."

He pulled a joint out of his pocket. "Well you better make up for lost time hadn't you?"

I couldn't find an argument with his logic. "Well I only promised no LSD, he didn't say anything about other drugs."

"At a boy." He lit up and after taking a deep drag, passed it to me.

I took it from him, but it felt uncomfortable in my fingers, I've never been a smoker. I took a deep drag, meaning to hold it back, but I ended up choking and coughing my guts up. "Jesus!" I spluttered and coughed as Sid was bent over double laughing at me. I passed it back to him while I finished bringing up a lung.

"Try not to take as much back this time." He passed it back to me.

I tried again. It still made me cough but not as bad as last time.

We sat for a while staring out at the ocean, listening to the screaming kids calling down the wind. "I don't think this is working Sid." I took another deep drag. I was getting used to this smoking lark now.

"Steady, it'll hit you in a minute."

He was right. Two minutes later and I could hardly talk. "SSSSSShhidd. Mmyy thhhong won't wourk."

Sid started laughing his arse off at me. "What? Your thong won't work?"

I peered up at him out of the slits that used to be my eyes. "I shhedd my tongue won't work."

"Fuck. How are you this shit-faced? You only had like three drags?"

I shook my head. Oo shouldn't have done that, the view in front of me kept shaking even after my head was still.

"Will you be okay to drive?"

"Drive what?"

"The car stupid." He shook his head in despair. "Fuck!"

"You drive." I pulled my keys out of my pocket and threw them at him.

"I can't drive."

"Course you can. I'll teach you. After I've finished throwi…." I vomited all over my shoes.

Sid half-carried me back to the car, and put me in the driving seat. He was hopping from one foot to the other. "You'll have to drive. I can't."

I tutted up at him and put the car into gear and shot backwards into a wall. That set me off laughing again. I'd need a new bumper from the scrap yard. Christ I was their best customer lately.

"Oh oh." I started laughing. "Sid ma boy, drive me home."

"God!" Sid fumed with his hands on his head. "I can't drive. I can't do gears!"

"We'll practise." I decided.

Across the road from us was an old cemetery that had a long winding driveway that ran down the centre of it. After engaging the correct gear this time I managed to get the car across to the cemetery without further mishap, bringing it to a stop at the entrance to the driveway. I looked up at the iron gates of the cemetery in surprise. There was an old wrought-iron archway high up above the gates - mostly made up of rust now. On the top of the archway was a motto in Latin. Half of the letters had rusted away leaving gaps behind. The letters now spelled out a new motto DAYNEJONNE.

I elbowed Sid. "Do you see that?"

"What?" He snapped.

"That." I pointed up. "What does that say to you?"

He shrugged. "Don't know. Half of its missing. Is it even English?"

"I think its Latin. But never mind. If you discount the missing letters what does it say?"

He screwed his face up. "Daynejonne."

"So I'm not seeing things."

"Hey I never said that."

That word haunted me. It itched my troubled brain.

"Come on then." Sid was getting impatient. "Are you teaching me how to drive or what?"

I shook myself out of my reverie. "Um, yeah."

He got into the driver's side and put his seatbelt on. He looked pretty nervous and gripped the steering wheel as if for dear life. From the passenger seat I showed him how to operate the clutch and gear lever, and tried desperately to explain 'biting point' but it fell on deaf ears. We bunny hopped up and down the cemetery drive before we had to come up with a new plan.

Actually the plan we came up with was great. Sid had no problem steering and braking, and I had no problem with gears. So we drove between us. When we needed to change gear, I simply yelled, "Clutch!" to Sid, who would depress it long enough for me to change up or down the gears. Trouble was, my stoned brain kept getting muddled up. I kept shouting 'Crutch', which would set us both off crying with laughing.

Sid was belly laughing at me when I got confused when I got it right, shouting "Clutch! I mean Crutch!" In confusion. He shook his head at me still giggling. "What a day."

So two stoned and giggling schizophrenics drove home in style.

Chapter Twenty-Two

Once Sid had dropped me off back at home he set off back to his B&B on foot. I was glad to be alone for a while; I was tired out from the full belly, fresh sea air, and the vast amount of skunk currently circulating through my respiratory system. A nap was in order I thought.

As I passed the hallway phone I remembered the strange phone call I received earlier. Did that really happen, or did I imagine it? I wasn't sure. I decided to press 1471 to see if I got through to the strange caller again. The number that was spoken to me by the robot at the other end was Linda's work number. That was right, it was Linda who rang.

I felt better then. I must have imagined it was someone else. I put the receiver down and went upstairs for a nap.

I didn't wake up until Linda came in later on that night.

"Hey sleepy head." She sat down next to me looking amused at my sleepy face.

"Sorry must have dosed off. I only meant to lie down for a bit."

"You must have needed it." She stood up. "Do you want something to eat? I've brought fish and chips in with me."

I bit my lip from telling her I'd already had some. Plus I was actually quite starving. "Sounds lovely."

"I'll go dish up then." She patted my leg and left.

I got out of bed and slipped my slippers on. Shit I'd have to pee before I did anything. I shuffled off to the bathroom yawning.

"Holy Fuck!" I exclaimed, as I saw the state of my eyes in the mirror. It was a good job it was dark when Linda came in. After I'd pee'd like a race horse, I had a good wash and woke up my tired blood-shot eyes. At least if Linda mentioned the state of them I could pretend I had gotten soap in them.

We sat on the couch in the living room eating our tea together and chatting. I asked after her dad.

"He's doing okay. Better than I expected actually. He said to say hello to you."

"Good. Tell him hello back when you next see him."

"I will." She paused while she finished eating. "I nearly forgot to tell you, I've got the number of a good hypnotherapist for you." She fumbled around in her jeans pocket before fishing out a business card. "One of my regulars went to him for hypnotherapy to stop smoking. He swears by him. What do you think?"

I took the business card in my greasy fingers. It said: -

Philip Manners MNCH (Reg) HPD
Hypnotherapy Specialist Consultant
Specialising in anxiety, depression, trauma, addiction,
memory problems, anger management, etc.

"What do you think?" She looked at me expectantly.

"I don't know. I don't know if I even believe in all this stuff."

"Will you at least give him a call and talk to him? He might be able to help."

Inwardly I bitch slapped her; outwardly I smiled and agreed I'd call him in the morning.

Thanks to the vast amount I had eaten and smoken, I was out like a light that night. No dreams of buses, terrorists, or goddam 'others'.

I woke up the next morning fresh and a daisy, full of the joys of summer until Linda reminded me that I had agreed to call the stupid fuck-faced, chicken-clucking, hypnothera-quack.

"The what?" Linda asked me.

"Sorry I didn't think I'd said that out loud." Shit!

"Chicken clucking?"

"You know, all that stage crap that they do making people think they're chickens and stuff."

She rolled her eyes at me with annoyance. "I'd pay to see you clucking round the floor like a chicken."

"We would be paying for it!"

"You promised you'd give it a try." The stern expression on her face silenced the mockery that I was about to unleash on her.

"Fine, I'll call."

"Good." She stood up twirling her car keys around her wedding finger. I could feel the involuntary spasm of my own wedding stump getting jealous of her normal digits.

"Are you coming to work today?"

"I might pop in a little bit later. I want to chill out for a bit, let the new medication take hold a bit more first."

"Okay." She kissed me on the forehead. "Ring me if you need me." She was almost out of the door when she called back, "Don't forget to ring the hypnotherapist."

"Yes Dear!"

Once she was safely out of the way I went over to the note pad next to the phone. Sure enough my doodles were still there from the day before. I took a closer look at what I had written. There was no mistaking it, in bold italics I had written 'Daynejonne'.

It was a puzzler. Surely it was just a coincidence? I sat down on the little chair next to the telephone table and looked closer at my doodles. What I had previously thought of as squares actually looked more like grave stones, and the flowers I had doodled looked more like offerings to the dead. Why would I have that cemetery on my mind?

I shook my head. Who knew? But while I was sat by the phone I might as well ring the chicken-clucking whatsit and see if he can help. I pulled the business card out of my wallet and dialled the number.

"Hello Philip Manners Hypnotherapy?" A polite lady answered.

"Er hello, my name is Flynn Locke, I don't know if you can help me, I'm looking for someone to help me with some, er, memory, issues?"

"We can certainly help you with that. Would you like to make an appointment? The first consultation is free."

"Yes, I suppose so. Thank you."

"No problem Mr Locke. How does Monday morning at ten o'clock suit?"

"Yes, that would fine."

"That's wonderful. Do you have our address?"

"Yes, I have it here on a business card."

"Splendid. Well that's all booked in for you Mr Locke, we'll see you on Monday morning."

"Okay, thank you love. Bye."

"Good bye."

I hung up the receiver with a sigh. I had certainly dragged myself into some bullshit here hadn't I?

I was awoken from my morose thoughts by the post dropping through the letter box. With a sigh I went off to collect the bills that it would no doubt consist of. I flicked through them, to find an official looking one for me. I tore it open with curiosity.

"Oh, my brain scan appointment, at last!" It was arranged for the following Tuesday. "God that's going to be a busy week. Chicken-clucking Monday, brain scan Tuesday, Thursday hospital. God when do I get a day off?"

I scowled as I stomped back through to the kitchen and chucked the rest of the post onto the table. Let cow-bag deal with them when she gets back later. I could feel the rage starting to spread up from my stomach and through my veins.

"Fucking fuck, fuck, fuck, arsewipe!" I bellowed as I stubbed my toe on the chair. "Bastard, stupid chair!" I picked it up and flung it at the kitchen wall. The shitting thing was mocking me, laying there on the floor all innocent like butter wouldn't fucking melt; so I picked it up and smashed it against the wall.

"That'll teach you." I told the pile of wood on the kitchen floor when I had finished. I stood there panting from the exertion, feeling much calmer by the minute, sloughing off the anger like a spent shroud.

"Shit!"

The broken chair I could replace before Linda got home, but the giant hole in the kitchen wall would definitely make her mad. "Oh god!" I put my hands over my head in despair. "What to do?"

Linda would freak out! She'd freak out and leave me. Why did I do it? *Again?*

"Get a grip." I told myself sternly. "Sid might come and help. He might know what to do." I fished my phone out of my pocket and dialled his number.

A sleepy voice answered. "Mmupphh?"

"Sid? It's me. Can you come round? I've got an emergency."

"Okay." He yawned. "Give me twenty minutes."

"Hurry." I put the phone down on him and turned back to the hole in the wall.

Sid looked terrible; he was trembling like a leaf. He always looked bit rough around the edges but today it was exacerbated by the ill looking person inside the grimy clothes. "I'm not so good." He told me.

"Sorry." I realised I had been staring and looked away.

"I think it's the lack of meds getting to me now. I ran out of Prozac the other day. All I've got left is the diazepam." He was really shaking badly.

I stepped over my wood pile and pulled open the kitchen drawer. From the back I pulled out my unneeded supply of Prozac. "Here."

"Thank god." He looked so relieved I thought he would cry. "Don't you need 'em?"

"No, I'm back on the proper stuff again now. It'll just take a bit of getting back into my system."

"Can I have a drink of water please?"

"Course. Or would you rather have tea?"

"Both. Water for the tablets, tea for the souls!"

I obliged him with the water, and put the kettle on.

Once he was medicated he looked a little calmer. "So what's been going on here then?" He looked around at my handiwork with amusement.

"The chair bit my toe so I killed it."

He nodded with amusement. "Good job. Very thorough."

"So what do I do now? Linda will have a fit when she sees this. I'm gonna be in serious shit."

"Well there's no doubt the chair's definitely dead, but the hole in the wall will take a bit of fixing won't it? Unless you just stick a picture over the hole."

I stared at him in disbelief. "Sid you're a genius! Of course we can cover it over. She'll never know will she?" I was delighted. What a simple fix for a catastrophic problem! I took down the large picture of a fruit bowl from the other side of the kitchen and test fitted it over the hole in the wall. "What do you think?"

He scrutinised it for a minute before nodding. "Yep that'll do it."

Once I had gotten a nail put in the wall I hung up the picture, happily seeing the hole in the wall vanish before my eyes.

"What about the chair?" Sid asked.

"That can go on the bonfire."

We carried all of the bits and pieces out to the bonfire I had made from the remnants of my broken shed. Finally, when we were finished, we could go get that well deserved cup of tea.

"You know Sid." I commented from over my tea cup. "I'm starting to think that we aren't that mad after all. Look how good we're getting at problem solving."

"True." He agreed. "I just wish we could solve the problem of where I put my Mother's body." He looked down sadly at his dirty hands.

"Well Rome wasn't built in a day." I didn't know what else to say. Certainly not 'I think I might have dumped her body somewhere in the Daynejonne cemetery'.

He sighed morosely. I decided to change the subject. "Did I tell you I've got to go see a hypnotherapist?"

"You're shitting me?"

"I shit you not. Linda's idea. She wants me to go get the bus incident wiped from my memory so that I stop having nightmares about it."

"Wow. Can they do that?"

"Don't know. I'll find out on Monday."

"What's your missus like?"

"Linda? She's wonderful."

"Really? You didn't sound very convincing there." He laughed.

He was right. If I couldn't convince myself that she was the wonderful woman I married, how could I sound convincing to others? "Okay, I'll level with you. But don't go getting the wrong idea. I know it's just me 'cause I've been messing about with the medication so much, but Linda seems really strange lately."

"Strange how?"

"Well, you know how we both have 'others'?"

"Yeah."

"There's an 'other Linda'. Everyone says it's my imagination, but I swear she's different lately. There's been times when I've really thought she might kill me."

"Why what's she been doing?"

"Nothing I can really put my finger on." I thought for a moment. "Her voice and her expressions don't match. It's like she's saying one thing with her eyes, but saying the opposite with her mouth. It's really confusing. Plus, I'm almost sure she hit me and knocked me out the other day. But I woke up in my van and she said I'd dreamed the whole thing."

"Weird. Has she always been like this?"

"No. Well, only when my medication isn't working." I laughed nervously. "So I know deep down it's just me. But that doesn't make it feel any less real."

"You'll get better now you're back on your pills." He nodded sagely.

"I know."

Chapter Twenty-Three

If Linda had noticed the gaping hole in the wall behind the newly placed picture she didn't say anything. She also didn't mention the missing fourth chair from the table - much to my relief. In fact, she seemed positively charming. She cooked me my favourite dinner, (Steak with pepper sauce.) She rented my favourite film on blue-ray, (The God's must be crazy). In fact, she was so nice and sweet to me I was starting to feel terrible for all the bad thoughts I had been having about her.

I caught her eye as she placed my meal in front of me. She smiled at me with the whole of her soul. Sunshine beaming out from her smile that I knew was only for me.

"I love you." I told her.

"Not as much as I love you." She squeezed my leg under the table.

"Careful, any more of that and all this dinner will be wasted."

She laughed seductively. "Later. Eat your tea."

I did, and it was delicious.

Later on after the film had finished, we were cuddled up on the sofa together when I picked up the hand that was resting against my chest and kissed it. "So why have I had the special treatment tonight?" I kissed her open palm again.

She sat up a little to look at me properly. She peered through her lashes at me like a little girl. "Actually, I am buttering you up a little."

"Okay, what for?"

She sat up straight and rested both her hands on my knee caps. "I don't want you to freak out or anything, 'cause believe me, it's good news."

"Okay." I was still worried.

"Well you know I've been a little moody recently, a bit up and down?"

"I hadn't noticed." Ouch that was a massive Pinocchio lie!

"Really? Maybe I haven't been as bad as I thought then. Anyway, there's been a very good reason for it." She reached out and held my hands with her eyes shining. "I'm pregnant."

I didn't understand. "How?"

She looked at me incredulously. "How do you think?"

"Good god." I fell into my own thoughts. "I thought we couldn't have any? I thought after the last miscarriage the Doctor's said it could never happen again?"

Her smile had faded a little. "Aren't you happy? It's a miracle."

"Course I'm happy." I lied. "It's just a shock."

"You don't look very happy." She folded her arms crossly.

"I'm sorry." I hugged her. "I'm delighted. It's just unexpected isn't it? Have you done a test?"

"Yes, three months ago."

"Three months ago? How far along are you?"

"Sixteen weeks."

"Sixteen weeks? And you're only just telling me now? Oh my god, I can't take this in." I stood up and started pacing up and down.

"I didn't want to get your hopes up. That's why I didn't tell you. We've never gotten past eight weeks with the other pregnancies. I wanted to be sure."

I started to calm down a little. "Is everything okay this time?"

She smiled up at me. "Everything is perfect this time."

I nodded, staring back at her, shell shocked.

"You're gonna be a daddy." she giggled.

"I'm gonna be a daddy?" I started to smile despite myself. I liked the sound of it. I liked the way it rolled off my tongue.

Daddy.

I turned to her with misty eyes and a lump forming in my throat. "Why aren't you fat?"

She laughed like mad at me. "I'm only showing a little bit. Baggy clothes hide it well."

"Oh. I just thought you'd gotten frumpy in your old age."

She thumped me with a cushion. "Old age?" She laughed. "I'm six months younger than you, you old git." She hit me again laughing. I loved that laugh.

We sat back against the sofa happy.

"It's gonna be a fresh start for us this you know." She smiled.

"Oh yes. Shitty nappies by the dozen, baby puke, midnight feeds…" I teased.

"You know you'll love it."

"I will. I can't take it in. I feel like I'm going to wake up in a minute."

"Trust me, you're wide awake." She looked away slightly. "This is why I wanted you to go see the hypnotherapist, to get all the negativity out, make room for the good things that are going to come."

I kissed her on the top of her head. "I'm booked in for Monday morning."

"Oh that's brilliant. Thank you so much for trying."

"It's the least I can do."

We sat smiling into the silence for a while longer.

"Have you thought of any names?" I suddenly wondered.

She looked thoughtful. "If it's a girl, I quite like Eve."

"Eve." I rolled it round my tongue. "Eve, Evie. Yes I like that. What about if it's a boy?"

"I don't' know. Boy's names are tricky, what do you think for a boy's name?"

"Sid."

"Piss off."

"I like it. If we have a girl you can call her Eve, if you have a boy, I can call him Sid."

"To be continued!" She laughed and led me off to bed.

I was getting used to the idea of a baby rather quickly. It was something new, something wonderful, a fresh start. Linda was positively glowing, I didn't know why I couldn't see it straight away before. It was so obvious she was pregnant. I only had to look at her radiant face to see it.

I went in to work with her on the Saturday and made a complete nuisance of myself. I wouldn't let her lift so much as a watering can. She kept slapping my hands away laughing every time I tried to grab something off her.

"Look I'm just trying to look after you." I argued when she threw me out.

"If you want to make yourself useful, go buy me some maternity clothes. I'm getting too fat for ordinary clothes."

I threw her a dirty look. "You must be joking!"

"I'm not." There was a definite twinkle in her eye. She was mocking me.

I decided to call her bluff. "That's fine. Anything you want."

She watched me with interest. "You need to go to *Mothercare*."

"I gathered that."

"I also want some maternity underwear." She was waiting for me to cave.

I met her eyes with an unwavering stare. "What size?"

We eyeballed each other like a pair of old cowboys about to embark in a gun fight.

"Size ten."

"Fine." I felt the bead of sweat rolling down towards my eye. I shook my head to flick it away while still maintaining a degree of manliness.

"See you later!" She called smugly to me as I left.

I text Sid from the car.

Fancy coming clothes shopping?

He text straight back.

Yeah, bored shitless might as well.

I smiled and set off to get him.

"This is not fucking funny!" Sid exclaimed from behind a stack of plus-size pants.

"Don't be a baby." I tutted, while inwardly hoping the shop assistant didn't think either Sid or I were transvestites. By the dirty looks she kept shooting over our way I believe that was exactly what she thought.

"I can't let Linda think I'm not mature enough to buy her underwear."

"You aren't mature enough, that's why you're paying me to go to the checkout with them."

"I'm not paying you to answer back." I had already picked out a couple of hideous maternity dresses that I thought might be adequate, if not let her come and do her own damn shopping.

Sid was just trying a pair of navy blue pants against his body to see how big they were, when a young woman walked passed and tutted at him.

"They're not for me." He called after her blushing.

I laughed my arse off at his reddening face.

"God!" He fumed and threw them back on the stack.

"These'll do." I said picking up a pair of size tens off the rack.

"Oh my god!" Sid called out. "You have to get her one of these."

I looked up to see him holding up a nippless nursing bra.

"Look!" He said with delight. "Peephole bra!"

I snatched it off him twanging the elastic as I did it. "Nursing bra stupid."

"Hey what's good for the baby's good for the baby maker."

"True." I considered it. "Stick it in the basket quick."

"What size is she?"

"I don't know." I held my hands up over my chest as if I was holding a pair of oranges. "This size?" I shrugged.

Sid had a look through the rack before pulling one out. "This size seems to have the most in stock, this must be the most average size or something. What do you reckon?"

"It'll do. Let's get the hell out of here."

We decided to go and get a cuppa on our way home, from the lovely coffee shop that Susan and I had been to the week before. Sid breathed in the heady aroma as we walked in through the front door. "God that must be what Heaven smells like."

I agreed and went to order while Sid picked out a table.

I smiled up at the waitress who always spoke to Linda and I when we came in. She seemed decidedly cool with me today. Was it just me or was she avoiding looking at me? After she ignored me for the second time, another waitress came over and served me. I shook my head, baffled at the cool reception I had received, picked up my tray and carried it over to the corner table that Sid had picked out.

"Thanks." He said gratefully as I handed him a cup of tea and a muffin.

"Welcome, and well deserved after queuing up and buying that peephole bra."

"That was one of the most embarrassing moments of my life." He groaned.

I smiled down into my coffee.

"So what do you make of this baby lark then?"

"I can't believe it to be honest with you. I put all ideas of babies out of my head years ago, but I'm really pleased."

He smiled bemused and shook his head. "Rather you than me."

"Don't you want kids then?"

"Never really thought about it to be honest. Maybe in another life I would have, but with my history, I'd probably be better off having the snip."

That made me wince a little.

He noted my wince with amusement. "So is that why she's been acting weird then? Hormones?"

I nodded. "It makes sense now. I don't know why I didn't realise sooner."

"Yeah well your head's been messed up hasn't it."

"Understatement of the year Sid."

"Yeah well, at least you've got good shit to look forward to now. Unlike me, all I've got to look forward to is the inside of a mental ward."

"Don't say that. Things might not get that bad."

He looked at me incredulously. "What you think they're just gonna forget that I may or may not have killed my mother?"

"Sorry." Shit I was handling this terribly. How had the conversation suddenly got this heavy?

"It's okay." He sighed deeply. "Well things can't get any worse, right?"

Twenty-Four

Monday morning found me in the waiting room, looking at the clock and waiting for the hypnotherapist to come and brainwash me when he was finished with another patient. I thought it was all a load of bullshit. But I had promised my wife, so here I was.

The receptionist kept looking over at me and smiling, I think she fancied me. A week ago I might have smiled back, flirted a little. This week however, I had a pregnant wife that loved me, so the receptionist could fuck off. I looked away out of the window.

Twenty minutes after my appointment time, I was summoned through to the mental torture chamber. The hypno-whatsit didn't look anything like I expected. He only looked about twenty-five, in a grey pin-striped suit that looked at least a size too small.

"Mr Locke." He held out his flaccid hand to me as he led me through to his office.

"Flynn."

"My name is Philip. Good to meet you. What can I do for you today?" He beckoned me to sit down.

"Well, this was my wife's idea. I don't really know if you can help or not."

"Try me. As my receptionist told you on the phone, today is a free consultation. I am a licensed practitioner, I promise I won't make you cluck like a chicken or bark like a dog. That's not how hypnotism works." He laughed to try and put me at ease.

It didn't.

He carried on. "If I don't feel like I can help you I will be honest and tell you so."

"Good to know."

"So how can I help?"

I paused trying to gather my thoughts. "I was on a bus that was blown up by a suicide bomber." I held up my mangled left hand for proof before continuing. "I was left brain-damaged too. My wife says I'm traumatised by the things that I saw. Actually, she's right, I am. I put it out of my head most of the time, I can go a whole day without thinking about it, but at night I have horrific nightmares. Mostly I can't remember them as soon as I've woken up, but lately since I've had a medication change, I'm starting to remember them."

He looked at me without commenting, so I carried on to fill the silence.

"They're terrible, awful dreams, part memories, part delusions I think."

He was still looking at me without commenting. Fuck him I'd had enough of talking. I decided just to stare back at him until he spoke to fill the silence.

It worked.

"I think I can help. I take it you want help to stop dwelling on the memories, subconsciously?"

"Yes."

He nodded. "Yes I'm sure I can help. I won't be able to make you forget completely, but I can make you more able to cope with them. Could you come back on Wednesday morning, at the same time?"

"I suppose."

"Excellent. I have had successes with cases similar to yours before. I can't go into details obviously, but I have had victims of violence and abuse come to me for help to rid them of negative thoughts and nightmares. I believe I can make things much easier for you."

"Well it's worth a try." Shit. Walked into this pile of bullshit hadn't I?

He bored the tits off me for another twenty minutes with all the ins and outs of it. But to be honest I switched off and just nodded in what I thought were the right places.

I agreed to go, I never agreed to listen.

In fact, the way I was falling asleep listening to him made me think he could quite possibly hypnotise me. Who knew?

I went back to the garden centre to tell Linda what a good boy I had been. I'd sat through the hypno-quack's bullshit without insulting him once, and I had agreed to go back on Wednesday.

She seemed pleased with me, she said she was anyway, but she seemed a little distracted. Probably a hormone thing I decided.

After deciding I wasn't needed for the day I went home. I was feeling a bit of a mood swing coming on and didn't want to end up taking it out on Linda. Although I was stressed, I patted myself on the back for recognising the warning signs. This was new. Normally I got no warning at all; I just believed that people and objects were going out of their way to antagonise me. Shit, I must be getting better!

Once I'd had something to eat and had a nap, I was fine again. Yep, I was definitely getting better. Dr Patel had been right about the new medication, I was able to handle the mood swings without being completely numb. Just the brain scan to get through now.

The following day, once again I was waiting impatiently at the hospital to have my head examined. At least I was in a different part of the hospital to normal, so it made a bit of a change. Plus the nurses here were much nicer to me. I suppose because none of them had ever been hit by a flying chair or rugby tackled as the other nurses that knew me had.

I was waiting for ages for my MRI. I don't know exactly how long as there was no clock on the wall and I'd forgotten to put my watch on, but it felt like I waited around for at least a couple of hours. To pass the time a little I even found myself making small talk with some of the other patients in the waiting room. I was definitely getting better; usually I would pretend to be deaf and dumb if someone tried to talk to me that I didn't know. Yet here I was instigating the small talk!

I told the bored looking young woman next to me all about my upcoming fatherhood. I think I must've annoyed her though as she kept making excuses to use the toilet every time I started up a conversation with her. When I gave up trying with the ignorant bitch I made the mistake of talking to the old man across from me.

"What?" He bellowed when I observed that it was very warm out today.

"I said it's very warm out today!" I shouted.

"What's worn out?"

"Never mind, doesn't matter!"

He grumbled under his breath and looked away. Or rather, he thought he grumbled under his breath, he actually said quite loudly. "Bloody mumbler!"

Charming! I thought.

It wasn't long after that when I was finally called through and had my head placed in the metal coffin.

"Try and relax Mr Locke." The young nurse said.

"You must be joking! Relax with my head in a giant microwave?"

She laughed softly. "It's not a microwave. Just try and relax and keep as still as you can for the next twenty minutes."

Actually it wasn't that bad, the humming of the machine through the headphones they had given me was quite hypnotic. After five minutes I was almost asleep. I was quite surprised when the twenty minutes was up and I was freed from the coffin.

"Is that it?" I asked.

"That's it. All done."

"So what happens now? Do I get the results today?"

"No, but I have a note here from your Doctor, Dr Patel asking for the results to be rushed through so that he has them for your appointment on Thursday."

"Oh, okay. Does that mean I can go home now?"

"It does."

When I switched my phone back on outside I found four texts from Sid. I flicked down and read the oldest first.

I think I'm being watched.
Can you come get me?

Odd. I flicked to the next one.

I shit you not I am being watched.
Where are you?

On to the third text.

It's the police, I'm sure of it.
Get here will you Goddam it!

My heart sank as I opened the last text.

They won't take me alive.

I drove as fast as I could to the B&B, expecting to see an armed siege outside. I thought there would be a swat team; the road would be cordoned off with police tape with 'crime scene' written across it. What I didn't expect to see was the boring hum-drum suburban landscape that was slowly crawling past me. Where were the police?

The closest thing I could see to 'authority' was a doddering old traffic warden across the road from me. I pulled up outside the B&B, well within the white lines of the parking bay. I eyeballed the traffic warden just to make sure he knew I had parked legally, and I knew it.

Once he was sufficiently uncomfortable with my stare, I ran up the path to the front door and found it unlocked. Good. Small mercies. I ran up the three flights of stairs to Sid's room. I found it at the end of the darkened hall, and pounded on the door.

Nothing.

I tried the handle. Locked.

"Sid!" I bellowed, hammering on the door with my fists. "Sid! Open up, it's me."

The manager came bounding up the stairs to see what the hell I was doing.

"I need to get in there." I pointed to the door. "Do you have a key? I think he may have hurt himself."

With that, the nervous looking manager produced a key from fumbling hands off the key chain hanging from his pocket.

"Allow me." I said stealing the key off him before he had chance to say no. I unlocked the door and shot in.

"Sid!" I called around the empty room. "Shit. Where is he?" I said to myself more than the manager.

"Bathroom?" The nervous Manager offered meekly.

I hadn't noticed the door behind me in the corner. I tried the handle. It wasn't locked and opened easily. As the door swung open, I saw the blood pouring out over the pink carpet below the bath tub, staining it forever red.

"Sid!" I cried with horror at the small figure slumped in the bath, bleeding profusely from both wrists. "Ambulance!" I barked at the puking manager who had just lost his lunch over the carpet in the corner.

"God Sid no! What have you done?" I tore off my t-shirt and vest and began trying to stem the bleeding, I was sure it was too late, but shit on a cracker I was gonna try.

"Sid! Can you hear me? Sid. Sid. Sid! Wake up!" I slapped his cold pale face hard.

No response.

"Sid! Goddam it Sid wake up!"

Nothing.

Wait, I had a brain wave. "Bobby! Bobby, wake up, can you hear me? Bobby? Bobby wake up. Wake up right now!"

His eyelids fluttered slightly.

"Bobby!"

He opened his eyes. His eyes stayed fixed on mine as I tried to reassure him that help was coming.

A lone teardrop rolled down his cheek as he said. "Sssssssorry."

Chapter Twenty-Five

I now had first-hand experience of what I had put Linda through so many times. The feelings of horror and helplessness - not to mention the guilt, were gut wrenching.

I vowed there and then in that ambulance with Sid/Bobby, that never, ever again would I try to take my own life. It was a selfish, needless, wasteful act. I never had so much respect for life as I did in that moment when he opened his eyes.

I went with him in the ambulance and held his hand all the way. Although I did feel the need to tell the paramedics that we weren't poofs or anything.

He laughed and said, "You mean you're not gay. Poof is an offensive word now."

"Sorry, I'm not good with political correctness." I shrugged. Perhaps he was a poof? Sorry, gay. Who knew?

I was asked many, many questions at the hospital about Sid/Bobby. For instance, I was asked about sixteen times if his name was Sid or Bobby. I just answered "Yes." Every time.

"Does he have any other name?" The paramedic had asked me.

I had to think about it to try and remember. "'Other' names are Pat, and devil man." Wow that was well remembered.

He gave me a funny look, but at least he left me alone after that.

So here I was, again! Another hospital waiting room, watching the clock on the wall ticking away the last few drops of my patience. In the end I decided to curl up into a ball across two of the seats and went to sleep.

Sometime later I was woken up and told that I could go see Bobby/Sid now. I was led down the corridor and into a single room where a tiny person who resembled Sid was laid out in the bed. He had lots of wires and tubes running in and out of him which alarmed me greatly.

"Is he going be okay?" I asked the nurse who had escorted me.

"We've given him a large blood-transfusion, and repaired his wrists. He's going to be okay. Thanks to you Mr Locke. You saved his life by binding his wrists like you did. If he'd have lost any more blood, he wouldn't be here now." She patted me on the shoulder and left with a kind smile.

I walked over towards to the bed, observing his name written on the wall 'Bobby/Sid'. That made me smile a little. "Sid?" I whispered softly. "Are you awake?"

"No." He sounded grumpy.

I heaved a sigh of relief. "Are you going to be okay?"

He opened his eyes wearily. "I feel like shit."

"You look like shit."

"Some fucking friend you are!"

"I never thought I'd be so glad to hear your whinging."

He sniggered a little. "Don't, it hurts if I laugh."

"I'd tickle you - you bastard if the paramedic didn't already think we're a pair of poofs!"

"He thought we were gay? Why what did you do to me?"

"Held your hand in the ambulance."

He groaned. "God! Did you have to?"

I thought about it. "It felt like the right thing to do."

He slumped his head back down on the pillow with a sigh. As he did - he looked up at the sign on the bed above him and started laughing. "Bobby/Sid. Fancy writing that on my chart!"

"As soon as they know you're awake they're gonna' want to know your real name you know?"

"I know. To be honest, I'm sick of running. I'm gonna' tell them the truth, tell them I don't know if I killed her or not. I can't keep running and hiding like this."

"But what about the nut-house?"

"It can't be any worse than being dead can it? And that's what's going to happen if I don't get the right medication. I'll get paranoid and do something stupid."

"Why did you do it? - Slit your wrists?"

He looked up at the ceiling wistfully. "I thought the police were outside closing in on me."

"It was a traffic warden."

"You're kidding me?"

"No. I saw him outside the B&B."

"That just proves my point exactly. I would have died for a traffic warden."

I shook my head. I didn't know what to say. No one should be sacrificed for those wankers.

"Don't worry." He said. "I'll keep you out of it. I won't let on about you having coffee with her the day she died. The last thing I want is to bring shit to your door."

I couldn't help but feel relieved.

He carried on. "You go home now, get some rest. You look worse than I do."

I didn't.

"On your way out, would you ask the nurse to come in and see me? I want to give her my real name and address."

I smiled at my brave friend, and left to do as I was bid, before going home to my wife.

The following morning I rang the hospital to see how Sid was, but was told that he was currently being interviewed by the police.

Shit my stomach dropped at the 'P' word.

Never mind, I would put it to the back of my thoughts for now. I had important bullshit to attend to. I had to be HYPNOTISED!

Chapter Twenty-Six

"Hello again, Flynn. If you'd like to get yourself comfortable on the couch, I'll be with you in a moment." Without giving me chance to reply he left through the door to waiting room.

I huffed and sat down on the couch. Get comfortable he'd said. How comfortable? Do I take my shoes off? Get undressed? Can I fart?

I played it safe and just stretched out with my feet up on the couch and waited.

I looked at the fish tank across the room that I was now facing. I gathered it was supposed to be relaxing. It probably would have been if not for the dead Neon Tetra floating about near the surface being pecked at by some hungry looking guppies. I looked away. I had enough stress without worrying about fish.

The door opened and in came Mr Clucking quack face. "Sorry about that Flynn. Good, I'm glad to see you've got yourself comfortable." He sat in a wheelie chair and wheeled it over towards me. "Before we start do you have any questions?"

I shook my head. "No, I think you covered everything last time. I know what to expect."

"Good, good." He paused for a few moments; trying to get himself into 'the zone' I took it. "Now Flynn, please close your eyes."

I obliged him. At least I didn't have to see the dead Neon Tetra now.

"I want you to listen to the sound of my voice, you are in a safe place, and nothing here can harm you. I want you to take a deep breath and relax, exhaling slowly."

Oh yeah this was really fucking relaxing.

"I want you to imagine that you are on a beautiful beach. The sun is high in the sky, and you can feel the rays of sunshine warming you as you stand on the beach. You can feel the sand beneath your feet, warm and smooth. You dig your toes into the sand it feels so nice under your feet. You start to hear the birds calling in the distance, a soothing peaceful call. Now I want you to walk down the beach towards the sun, and find a comfortable place to sit. Anywhere you like as long as it's comfortable."

In my mind, I settled myself onto the rock Sid and I had shared on our day at the seaside.

"Now I want you to get yourself comfortable, relax, let your whole body sink down into your seat. From your comfortable seat I want you to watch the ocean, I want you to watch the waves rolling in and out, lapping at the beach. As each wave rolls in I want you to breathe in, and as each wave rolls out to sea, I want you to exhale."

I could feel myself sitting on the rock in the sunshine, I was immensely relaxed.

"Now I'd like you to watch the sun high up in the sky. As I start to count backwards from ten, the sun is going to get lower and lower in the sky. As the sun gets lower and lower, your breathing will get deeper and deeper, making you more and more relaxed with every breath. By the time I get to one, you will be in a suggestible state of consciousness.

Ten, you notice the sun is a little lower.

Nine, your heart rate slows a little.

Eight, you start breathing slower and deeper.

Seven, you become aware that your body is getting heavier.

Six, you are feeling sleepy.

Five, the sun is much lower in the sky now.

Four, every muscle in your body is relaxed.

Three, you feel very safe.

Two, sun is almost set.

One, the sun has gone down, and you are in a semiconscious state.

You are in a safe place. Nothing here can hurt you, I want you to visualise a television in front of you now. You are in charge of what you watch on the television, you are in control. However nothing on the screen can harm you, I want you to describe what you see on the screen without feeling any emotional distress at the images you to see."

I looked up from my rock to see an old television set sat next to me. It was one of those old things from the eighties, green concave screen surrounded by a huge mahogany case. Giant push buttons down the right-hand side of it.

"I want you to watch the screen closely. There have been things that have happened in your past that have been bothering you. On the count of three, I want you to watch these events play out on the screen in front of you. Once you have watched the events on the screen, you are going to reach out with your hand and press the delete button on the side of the TV."

As he spoke I noticed the big red delete button on the left-hand side of the TV.

"On the count of three you are going to watch the events that are bothering you, but you are watching from a safe place, nothing can hurt you or worry you, you will not feel any distress or anxiety. Now on the count of three the TV is going to start, I want you to describe to me what you see. One, Two, Three."

The TV sparked to life. I could see the grainy image of the bus start to appear. Then the picture faded until it melted into an image of Linda and myself on board. I could see Linda's lips moving as if she was speaking to me, but I couldn't hear her voice. She looked excited as she turned to look out of the front window of the bus. I turned with her, standing slightly behind her with my hands around her waist. I laughed into her hair as I nuzzled her neck. Suddenly I looked around, grabbing the metal support bar behind me with my left hand as I heard something. A man was standing up in the aisle shouting something before fiddling with a device in his hand that could have been a phone, I wasn't sure.

The violent intensity that the wave of fire brought with it was mind shattering. I could see the events in slow motion. I saw people explode. I saw parts of people hit other people. The 'me' on the bus fell over as the fingers that were holding onto the metal support bar disintegrated. I saw my head fly backwards and hit a support stanchion. I could see Linda from the comfort of my rock, unconscious behind me from hitting the windscreen, shielded by my body. Before the 'me' on the bus blacked out from the massive head injury I had received, I felt the sensation of boiling blood hitting my bare leg.

"Tell me what you see Flynn." The voice came from the heavens into my ears.

"I see the explosion on the bus. I see everything. The bomber, the fire, the bodies. All of it."

"You're doing wonderful Flynn. The image you just saw will never bother you again. You may think of it from time to time, but it will never upset you again. I want you to reach out now and press the delete button on the side of the TV. Can you do that for me?"

"The TV hasn't finished yet."

Suddenly the image on the screen had changed. I was watching myself inside the back of my van. I was covered in blood and there was a body of a woman. It looked like I was crying and saying something. I desperately wanted to know what I was saying.

As I thought this I noticed a volume knob on the TV so I reached out to turn it up. Instantly I heard the INXS song start up deafeningly loud. ….

"Don't ask me, what you know is true. Don't have to tell you, I love your precious heart…."

.I was holding the bleeding woman and crying, I watched myself sob and say. "I'm so sorry. I had no idea. I knew it wasn't just me."

I watched myself turn to the driver of the van. "I'll kill you for this!"

"Flynn? What do you see?" The hypnotist wanted to know.

"I want to get out."

"Get out of what?"

"The van."

"What van?"

"My van."

"Tell me what's happening."

"I can't." I started crying.

"You're safe Flynn, you can tell me anything."

"Let me out!"

"Flynn, nothing can hurt you."

"No, but I can hurt you. Shall I tell you about the dead woman in my van?" I looked up from the couch with as much menace as I could. "Let me OUT!"

I could see him looking nervous at me. I glared at him, daring him.

"I'm going to count to ten now, and when I get to ten, you are going to come out of the suggestive state and feel much more positive."

I could hear the fear in his voice as he started reciting his bullshit on auto pilot.

"One, Two, Three, Four, Five, he started speeding up, Six, Seven, Eight, Nine, Ten!"

I sat up and eyeballed him. "Can I go now Doc?"

He nodded.

Once I got outside I vomited into the gutter.

I remembered.

I should have known. 'Other me' had been trying to remind me about it by playing that song at me constantly. I thought he was taunting me, he wasn't. He was the 'me' that could remember what had been brain-washed out of me.

I walked down the street to where I parked the van. As I reached for the handle I felt sick. I couldn't get into that thing. It was out of the question. Never, ever again would I get back inside that thing. What to do?

I couldn't afford a taxi; I had given all my money to the receptionist of the hypno-quack. All I had was a pocket full of change. I couldn't call Linda, when she asked why I was distressed what could I tell her? She'd see right through me if I lied, she'd know it was something major and she'd get it out of me. I sat on the edge of the fountain at the edge of the park, a few hundred yards from where I had left the van. I needed to think.

What could I do? Linda was four-months pregnant. With her history of miscarrying I didn't dare bring up any of this shit that had come hurtling back into my brain. I couldn't put that kind of risk on my child. I couldn't go home. One look at my face and that would be it. EVERYTHING would come out.

I pondered it for a while. Linda would be going straight to her dad's from work, so if I just kept out of the way for a while till she'd gone, I could go home and pretend to be asleep when she got home. Then in the morning I could 'accidently' sleep in and not get up until after she'd gone. Yes, that sounded more like a plan. It would buy me some time before I'd have to face her. But, she's going to want to know how I got on at the hypno-do-da, shit. She said she'd pop home to see me afterwards. SHIT!

I know, I'll text her and tell her it went well, but I can't ring her 'cause the signal here is crap. Yep, that would have to do. I pulled my phone out.

Hey Linda,
Hypnotherapy was great. No problems,
Memory wiped lol.
Can't ring u, got crap signal. See u tonight.
xxxx

That would do it. I thought it sounded light enough. I was just putting the phone back into my pocket when it beeped.

Glad u got on ok.
Can't wait to hear.
See u tonight, can't get home this afty,
too busy. But love you xxxx

I exhaled, and replied that I loved her too.

I put my phone away and looked down at the change in my hand. It was no good, I would have to break the cardinal rule and get the bus home. It was something that I would never entertain normally, but today buses were the last of my worries.

I hadn't been on a bus since 'the incident' and I expected to be terrified. I thought I'd start screaming and panicking, going demented to get off. But no.

I politely paid the driver and climbed the stairs to the top deck and sat at the front so that I could look at the panoramic view out of the window. I was fine. My heart-rate hadn't fluctuated, my breathing was regular, and I had no feelings of panic at all. Perhaps the hypno-wanker could work miracles after all?

I leant over to look down the little mirrored periscope and looked at the driver's bald head. Yes that definitely wasn't 'other me' driving.

I sat there trying to calmly rationalise the awful thing I had seen on the TV when I had been under. How reliable were these memories? I have read many times in the tabloids about people being planted with false memories while under hypnosis. Perhaps this was one of those occasions?

It wasn't. I knew it wasn't. I knew what I'd seen was real, what's more; I knew if I had carried on watching that screen, I would have seen a hell of a lot more. I had to talk to someone and share these thoughts. I knew I could be delusional so I would have to check that it isn't just me. I had my doctor's appointment in the morning; I would go and visit with Sid afterwards if I would be allowed in to see him. I could talk to Sid; I think he'd be okay; we needed to get our stories straight. I'd just have to get through the appointment with Dr Patel first, and more importantly, stay the hell away from my wife.

Chapter Twenty-Seven

I got off the bus at the stop nearest to my house. I mentally congratulated myself for the huge mile-stone I had just completed. If only my old doctor Dr Mandela could see me now!

"Thank you." I called to the driver as I got off.

I stood at the bus stop just watching the bus depart. I couldn't believe how easy it had been.

I think I had finally got the closure my poor damaged brain had been seeking. Now I just needed closure on the 'other matter'.

I let myself in through the front door and made my way through to the kitchen. I opened the drawer and pulled out the emergency stash of Diazepam I had saved. I believe that this qualified as a crisis. To be sure of a suitable numbness to get me through the next twenty-four hours, I pulled six out of the bottle. That should do the trick.

I made myself a cup of tea and settled myself down at the kitchen table to take my pills. As I was drinking my eyes were focused on the picture of the fruit bowl I had hung up over the hole in the wall. How had Linda not noticed it? Had she noticed it and let it go so as to not upset me? Wait a minute, I was assuming there was a hole behind the picture, but was there, or had I made it up?

I walked over to the picture to double-check, but as I reached my hand out to it, I chickened out. I didn't think I wanted to know if it was real or not. If I faced up to that, I might start having to examine if 'other things' were real or not. I shook my head and sat back down. I'd rather stay with my head in the sand.

It wasn't long before the Diazepam started making me sleepy, so I toddled off for a nap.

I must have slept for much longer than I had intended. I didn't wake up until I felt Linda get into bed beside me. "Flynn." She gently shook me. "Flynn? Are you awake Love?"

I ignored her and pretended to be asleep. In my sleepy state I might not be able to lie well enough to convince her. Best to avoid her till I got my head straight.

She gave up and cuddled up to my back. "I love you." She whispered into my hair.

She did, she really, really, did.

The next morning I awoke with an almighty headache. I could hear Linda banging about downstairs cooking breakfast. Ugh, the smell of the bacon frying was making me retch.

"Flynn?" She bellowed up the stairs. "Breakfast is ready!"

So much for hiding until she was gone. Now I'd have to get up and face her. "Alright!" I shouted down to her, grumpily pulling yesterday's clothes on from off the floor.

I looked in the mirror to see the 'other one' peering out at me with eyes like piss-holes in the snow. Never mind. I shook my head, not the day for vanity. I made my way down to the stinking dead pig smell coming from the kitchen.

"Morning Love," she called from the stove. She turned back around sharply after seeing my dishevelled appearance. "What's the matter? You don't look very well."

"I've got the worst headache in the world!" I moaned truthfully and sat down. "Do you mind if I skip breakfast? I feel a bit sick."

"Course I don't mind. Poor love. Do you want some headache tablets?"

I nodded.

"Here you go." She pulled them out of the drawer and set them down in front of me with a glass of water.

"Thank you." I swallowed them gratefully. "Sorry about ruining breakfast."

"Not a problem. All the more for me." She said winking at me cheekily, grabbing a piece of toast. "Eating for two remember!"

"Oh I remember." I tried to smile but I don't think it came out very well, as she looked away.

"Don't forget you've got your appointment today will you?"

"I haven't forgotten."

"I got a call from Dr Patel's secretary earlier asking me if I could come with you this morning. I said I would, but I just checked with Jennifer who covers for me, and she can't come in on such short notice. Would you mind making my apologies for me not being able to go with you after all?"

"Yep. I wonder why they want you there?"

She paused and swallowed hard. "I must admit I am a little worried. It's today you get the results of the brain scan isn't it."

I nodded.

"I'm sure it's nothing. Probably just want your carer's opinion on the new medication, how you're reacting to it or something."

"That's probably what it is. Dr Patel does seem to prefer talking to you rather than me."

She smiled, before remembering. "Oh god how did the hypnosis go?"

Shit! I was hoping she wouldn't mention that. "It was okay. Pretty much what you'd expect."

"How did you get back? I noticed the van's missing?"

Shit, brain think! I stared at her with a blank face until thankfully the answer was whispered into my brain. "I got the bus home."

"You what?" Her face fell.

I nodded. "I wanted to see if it had worked. - The hypno-doo-da. So I left the van and hopped on a bus."

She put her hands over her face. "I can't believe it. And how were you?"

"I was absolutely fine. I think I'm cured."

She smiled a true proper smile at me. Shaking her head in disbelief as she beamed. "You are so brave!"

"Well, I do try."

"I can't believe you've been on a bus!"

"It was no big deal." It was the least of my fucking problems.

"I've got to go to work now, but I want to hear all about it when I get back."

"I'll tell you everything."

Who knew the next time I saw her, I really would be telling her everything.

I walked into the hospital at my usual time (five minutes early), to find the waiting room empty. I looked about me in surprise. No other patients, screaming children, irate mothers. No nurses glaring at me from the wings, getting ready to duck from whatever I might throw at them. As my footsteps echoed around the room I felt as though I had entered the Twilight Zone.

My confusion was intensified when I spotted Dr Patel sitting on the first chair of the waiting room at the far side from me. He stood up as I approached him.

"What's going on? Have I got the wrong day?"

"I've been waiting for you Flynn. I've cancelled all the other appointments for today."

Shit. This was heavy. He knew, didn't he? Somehow, he knew.

"Where's Linda?" He peered around me.

I shook myself out of my trance. "Sorry, she couldn't make it. She had an emergency at work."

He pursed his lips with obvious annoyance. "Please come through to my office and take a seat." I allowed myself to be ushered through.

"Would you like something to drink? Tea or coffee?"

Bollocks! Something was really, really, wrong. In almost a decade of coming here I had never once been offered a drink. I better not let him see I'm nervous. I smiled and said a cup of tea would be nice.

He didn't return my smile.

While I was alone I allowed myself to quietly freak out. FUCK, FUCK, FUCK, FUCK, AND FUCK!!!!!!!! I hit myself on the side of the head in frustration.

By the time Dr Patel returned with my tea I had got a little more control back, and was nervously tapping away all seven fingers on the arms of the chair I was hoping I wouldn't end up throwing.

He slid the cup of tea over to me without a word, and sat down across from me. Watching me.

If he wanted a staring contest he could have one. I wasn't about to start talking first.

I won.

"Flynn, I have here the results of your brain scan." He paused for effect. "Frankly, I don't know how this can have happened in this day and age." He paused again, wool gathering as my mum would have put it. "Flynn, the MRI shows that you are NOT brain-damaged. I can find no trace of any damage to your brain whatsoever."

"What?" I was baffled. "Is this some kind of joke?"

"Believe me, it's no joke. I have had several other specialists check my findings, and all concur, you are not - and never have been, brain-damaged."

I sat in silence trying to absorb what I had just been told. It made no sense. "But I have mood swings, personality disorders, fucking anger problems!"

"Of course you do. You have been taking mind altering medication that you do not need for almost a decade. Anyone who didn't need medication like that would react in exactly the same way as you have."

"I don't understand."

"I believe you."

I looked up at him feeling panicky. "How did this happen?"

He gave me a wry smile. "I think I may know."

He opened two files up, and left them face up on his desk. He then turned back to me.

"After extensive research, I think I know what happened. This is a little tricky as I cannot legally discuss another patient with you without their permission. How can I put this without making myself liable?" He rubbed his eyes in frustration. "Two patients were brought in, in the same ambulance from the bus crash. One was brain damaged, one wasn't. They both had the same last name, and, almost the same date of birth." He nodded at me meaningfully. "Somehow, the results got mixed up, and the wrong person was diagnosed. Do you understand my meaning Flynn?" He stared at me again.

"I don't understand."

He sighed. "I'm going to pop out for a few minutes. Whatever you do, don't look at that file that's open on my desk, will you?" He pointed at it and nodded.

I caught his drift and nodded.

"Good."

He left. I leaned over and spun the two files around so that I could see them properly. My heart sank. There it was in black and white.

'F. Locke DOB 01/01/74. Admitted 07/07/05'
'L. F. Locke DOB 01/07/74. Admitted 07/07/05'

It was easy to see how they could have gotten muddled up. The 7 written on Linda's date of birth looked more like a One than a Seven, and the 'L' had got a staple through it, it was barely there. For all intents and purposes, the names and dates of birth were identical.

I exhaled sharply. I wasn't brain-damaged, and never had been. Linda was the brain-damaged one, and had been from the start.

Chapter Twenty-Eight

I slid the folders back the right way around and sat back in my chair, quietly trying to absorb all the information I had been given. My brain was whirling with it all.

The door opened and Dr Patel came back in. He gave me a sympathetic smile and sat back down at his desk, closing the files as he did so. "You see now why I wanted Linda to come with you today?"

I nodded.

"I'm afraid there is more yet that we have to discuss."

My heart sank a little further down into my stomach. I nodded that I was still listening.

"I have spent the last twenty-four hours going through every scrap of information that we have on you and the 'other' patient. I have interviewed several colleagues who have worked with you both over the years. And I'm afraid I am a little alarmed by the way the evidence is starting to add up." He paused and looked up at the ceiling. "It seems like I am not the only person who has come across this false information Flynn."

I looked up sharply. "What do you mean?"

"Your late doctor, Dr Mandela discussed a similar theory with the 'other patient' it seems, not long before she died."

By other patient I took it he meant Linda. I didn't like the way this was going.

He continued. "According to her former secretary, Dr Mandela arranged for an appointment to discuss this very idea with the 'other patient', but all record of this appointment seems to have vanished off the face of the earth. The only reason I know of it is because Dr Mandela's former secretary admitted to me that she had 'accidently' eavesdropped on the conversation between the two of them. The secretary said the exchange got quite heated between them. However, a week later Dr Mandela died, and the secretary didn't feel like she had the authority to bring up what she'd overheard. She had, after all been eavesdropping. She was worried about getting the sack due to a breach in patient confidentiality. It took a great deal of persuasion on my part for her to admit to any of it."

"So what does this mean?"

"It means that the 'other patient' knew the truth and yet did nothing about it. Do you get what I mean Flynn? The 'other patient' knowingly allowed you to be unnecessarily medicated. Despite knowing the truth."

"But why would she do that to me?"

"That is exactly what I want to know. Also, the secretary that we spoke of believes that she caught the 'other patient' in the records room going through the filing cabinet. She believes 'they' may have altered your epilepsy results. The secretary confirms that this was just after the test was carried out." He paused. "She also found the 'other patient' in the record room a few days after Dr Mandela died." I got his inference.

Good god this was getting more confusing by the minute.

"Flynn, the only legitimate thing that we know that is different about you since the 'bus incident' is the blackouts you say you suffer from. If you have no brain-damage, we can't blame left-frontal-lobe-syndrome anymore. You do not, and cannot have personality disorders. Can anyone else confirm the 'other one' as you call him, appearing during the blackouts? Has anyone but Linda ever seen your other, violent personality?"

I shook my head. "I only know about the 'other one' from Linda. When I wake up from a blackout she tells me what I've done." My voice was starting to wobble. Please don't let me cry here.

Dr Patel put his head in his hands in disbelief. "Just to confirm, Linda is the only one who has ever told you that you have another personality when you black out?"

"Yes."

"And you have no memory of these attacks when you wake up and the house is in disarray and Linda would be hurt."

"I don't remember any of it." It was getting difficult to speak through the lump in my throat.

"I understand how confusing and distressing this is for you. But everything is going to be alright. I am going to wean you down off all of the medication very gently. You have been on it far too long to just stop it all. You would become very distressed. You would quite probably become delusional; for certain you would have catastrophic mood swings."

I just nodded, not trusting my voice.

"Now I hope you understand just how important it is that your wife comes to see me immediately."

"I understand."

"I don't wish to involve the police if this matter can be straightened out quickly. But I must stress, this must be straightened out immediately!"

"I understand."

He seemed to accept me at my word, and turned back to his computer screen. "I'm printing you off a new prescription which I want you to start taking at once. The instructions for the new dosage will be written on the box. Also, I am requesting an epilepsy test for tomorrow morning. I sincerely believe that you are epileptic and that is what these so-called blackouts have been. I believe your results were altered to make us believe that you weren't epileptic for some nefarious
reason that I have yet to understand."

I shook my head. "For years I've been saying that I wasn't mad, it was Linda that was nuts. Nobody believed me." A tear slid involuntarily down my cheek.

"This is a lesson for all of us Flynn. So many times people are failed because their claims aren't taken seriously due to matters that are beyond their control."

"I knew she was different. I've spent nine years trying to convince myself that everything was in my head. Deep down I knew the truth. I knew she was crazy."

"Massive brain damage left untreated can leave people greatly altered. With the right medication, the 'other patient' will be much more normal and balanced. It will just take a while to get the medication right."

"She's pregnant. Will that mean that she can't have the medication yet?"

He paled slightly. "That would change things yes." He gave me a sympathetic pat on the arm. "Things will get better now." He paused. "I want to see you tomorrow morning, Nine o'clock for that epilepsy test. In the meantime, get Linda to come in as soon as possible. It would perhaps be wise to not discuss any of this with her, until I have seen her myself."

"Okay."

He stood up to show me out of the door. "Frankly Flynn, I'm staggered at how something like this can happen. I was shocked when I began working with you to find that you'd been discharged after the head injury after spending only two days in hospital. Perhaps if they had kept you in longer then the mix up would've become apparent. Only one brain scan in almost a decade is a disgrace." He shook my hand and closed the door as I left.

I needed to find Linda and have it all out with her once and for all. Bollocks to leaving it all to the doctor to sort out. I wanted answers. NOW!

I caught a bus outside of the hospital without even thinking about it. I paid my fare and climbed the stairs to the spot at the front with the panoramic views that I liked so much when I was a child. It would take around thirty-minutes to get to the garden centre by bus, but I didn't care. I needed to think.

All the times I had thought Linda was looking out for me, picking the quiet table in the corner away from the noise so that I wouldn't be bothered by people. Getting annoyed if I was left waiting too long. Turning down the TV to stop noisy adverts from driving me mad. It was all for HER. Not me. She was the one most bothered by noise, crowds, waiting. She convinced me it was all down to me. I couldn't believe it. Yet I could. The last time we had been at the hospital together she had been spitting feathers at us waiting past our appointment time. I believed she was reacting so that I wouldn't have to, as so many other carers' do for their patients. Wrong. She was the impatient one on the verge of a temper tantrum.

All my temper tantrums had been because of taking mind altering medication that I didn't need. I wasn't crazy, I didn't have 'anger issues' and I was NOT FUCKING BRAIN-DAMAGED!!!!

That bitch had a lot to answer for.

Chapter Twenty-Nine

I got off the bus without incident and made my way across the road to the garden centre. I wasn't sure exactly what I was going to say, but I knew as soon as I saw her everything would come bursting out. I pulled the door open and went inside. Normally the heat and humidity as I opened the door made me feel warm and comforted. Today it made me sick, sticky and angry.

I made my way over to the till where Jennifer was serving a customer. Jennifer only worked part time and wasn't supposed to be able to come in today, so Linda had said earlier anyway.

"Jennifer, where's Linda?" I didn't have time for hello's or pleasantries.

She looked up in surprise. "Hi, I thought she was going to the hospital with you? She asked me to cover for her while she went with you for your brain scan results."

"That lying bitch!" I snarled and turned back around and stormed off.

Where the hell was she? I slammed my way out of the doors and stood outside trying to think what to do. What was she up to? The only place I could think that she might have gone would be to her dad's. But why lie about it? I'd have to go and see if she was there. The only problem with that was that I now had no transport. Linda had the car, and I was frightened of the van. FUCK!

It was no good, I would have to go and get the van. Linda's dad lived too far away to get a bus or a taxi. I'd simply have to bite the bullet and drive the damn thing. I could always pull over and vomit if I had to.

I stormed back into the garden centre and went behind the till much to Jennifer's alarm and pulled a handful of bills out of the drawer. "Jen, we're closing for the day. I'll give you all this money if you'll just take me to town on your way home so that I can pick up my van."

She looked completely taken aback, but seemed to be leaning towards the 'he's nut's so I better do what he says' scenario. I felt like telling her that actually she could ask my doctor if she wanted, I'm NOT mad. But this wasn't the time or place.

She kept one eye on me as I locked the front doors up and handed her the money, (that she squirreled away quick enough.)

She drove like a lunatic all the way to town which made me cringe, but needs must, I had to get my transport back. I almost fell out of her car once we arrived at my destination. My knees had turned to jelly during the white-knuckle car ride.

Once I was poured out of her passenger seat, she drove off without a backwards glance. Never mind, I was here now. I went over to my van, staring in horror at the clamp that was hugging my back wheel. "NO!" I cried. "Not now! Ahhhh!" I sank to my knees in front of it.

"Flynn?" - A voice said from behind me.

I wiped my nose and turned around to see the Hypno-quack.

"Are you okay?"

I shook my head with tears pouring down my cheeks.

"Come on. Come with me. I've got a pot of coffee on the go in my office." He helped me up and half-carried me across the road to his office. I leant against the name plate on the wall while he fished his keys out of his pocket and let us both in. "Please sit. I'll make you a coffee."

"Thank you." I nodded gratefully. Here I was again, back on the couch staring at what was left of the dead Neon Tetra. I closed my eyes and waited for Philip to come back with my coffee.

"Here you go, get that down you." He put a cup down in front of me.

"Thank you."

He looked at me with concern as I took a sip. "Do you want to talk about it?"

I sighed. Did I?

"I'm sorry if I scared you yesterday. I didn't mean to. I was just having a panic attack. I remembered seeing something horrible that someone else had done."

He laughed nervously. "It's not every day that someone tells me they have a dead woman in their van." He fidgeted with his cup.

"I must have blocked it out. I can only remember little bits and pieces. But I know for certain that I didn't hurt her." I fell into my own thoughts for a while.

"Do you know who did?"

I nodded. "My wife."

"Your wife?"

"She's crazy. I thought it was me that was crazy, but it really isn't. It's her."

He looked shocked. "What are you going to do?"

"I'm going to confront her. Or rather I was, my van's been clamped."

"Don't you think you should call the police?"

"Not yet. I need to talk to her first. Then I'll call the police. I don't remember enough to go to the police yet."

"Well you're in the right place if you want to remember. Do you want me to put you back under? I only hypnotised you yesterday, it would be much quicker to put you back under now."

"You'd do that for me?"

"In light of what you have told me, I think it's my duty. Would you object to me filming the session? It might be needed as evidence."

God this was all getting a bit too real. "I suppose you're right. Yes, you better film it."

He nodded and started setting up his video camera.

I laid out on the couch trying to relax. All I felt was sick to the stomach.

Twenty minutes later, and I was back sitting on the rock on the beach, staring at the screen of the old eighties TV.

"Tell me what you see." Philip asked softly.

The grainy screen started to clear a little. I could see an image of the back garden of our house. It looked as though Linda and I were having an argument. I could see her gesturing with her fists as if to hit me. I could see me holding my hands up trying to calm her down. I couldn't hear what was happening so I reached out and turned the volume up a little.

I heard Linda screaming. "I saw you looking at that little bitch. You are MINE! You are not to go near that little cow again or believe me I will kill you both."

I watched myself trying to calm her down. "Linda, I don't even know who you're talking about. I would never look at anyone but you. You know I love you. Only you."

She threw me away with a snarl. "I'm not fucking stupid! I know what I saw." She hit me then with something. I think it was the paddle off our old canoe, but I couldn't be sure. The picture moved a little then.

Ah, this scene I had seen before. I was waking up in the back of my van covered in blood. I watched myself realise that there was another body in the back with me. I looked on in horror as I recognised the face of the daughter of our milkman, or rather what was left of her pretty face. She'd had her head caved in. As I started to scream, Linda turned the radio up to cover the noise. *INXS* blurted out from the stereo, Linda's favourite album.

Linda hissed at me to be quiet or she'd start screaming and tell people that I killed the girl. No one would believe me over her, she said.

I quieted my sobs, and tried to breathe and wake up; after all I must be dreaming. I looked around at my surroundings, it was dark, but we were parked under a street light somewhere. I looked out of the small back window to see that we were parked opposite a cemetery. 'Daynejonne' was spelt out over the wrought iron gates.

Linda hissed at me that she was going across the road to open the gates and that I was to stay quiet till she got back. She advanced on me with her bolt croppers, teeth flashing menacingly in the moonlight. I nodded that I would stay quiet. Once she was satisfied, she ran across the road and cut through the lock releasing the chain off the gates. She carefully opened them, one by one, before coming back to the van and driving slowly through them. She drove right to the back of the cemetery before parking up. "Get out!" She ordered me.

I complied. Too shocked to think for myself.

"Now dig!" She handed me a spade and pointed to a freshly dug grave next to the van. It was a recent burial, so the mud was fairly easy to dig through.

watched in horror from my safe place on the rock, at the image on the TV screen of Linda and I tipping the poor young girl into the hole I had dug. I remembered talking to that young girl a few times when she had been round collecting money for her dad. She was nice. I knew Linda didn't like her, she was jealous of the pretty young thing - though I didn't know just how jealous she had got, or rather, I had forgotten.

I related everything that I had seen to Philip, who had reassured me throughout that I was safe, and nothing could hurt or upset me. That wasn't true, but at least we had gotten through it.

He brought me back out of my trance and turned the camera off. As I opened my eyes I saw how white his face had gone. He was shaking his head, lost for words at what he had heard. He found his voice. "We have to call the police."

"We will, but not till I see her, I want to have it out with her, I think there might be more things that I don't know about."

"She's a murderer. You have to go to the police."

I shook my head. "Not yet. I know where she is, and I'm going to get it all out of her. If you don't hear from me by…four o'clock, call the police and send them to this address." I wrote her dad's address down on the pad next to the couch.

"Okay, but I'm not happy about it."

"Can I borrow your car?"

He threw his keys at me with a worried look.

Chapter Thirty

I let myself into Philip's BMW that had been parked opposite my van. After fiddling with the seat and the mirror I finally got comfortable enough to set off. As I pulled out of the parking bay I saw Philip staring after me from the rear-view mirror. I just hoped he'd keep his promise and not call the police just yet.

I manoeuvred carefully through the busy town traffic not wanting to damage Philip's car. Plus, my hands were shaking so much I didn't dare drive with my usual care free abandonment.

Once I was through town and out onto the B roads I relaxed a little and allowed my thoughts to flow.

When I had my first hypnotherapy session and I had seen Linda in the driver's seat of my van, I had half-wondered if she had been covering for me. After all, I was in the back covered in the dead girl's blood. I hadn't seen enough on the TV screen to realise the extent of Linda's behaviour. I remember waking up in bed the morning after Linda killed the girl. Linda had been covered in bruises and scratches and was sitting whimpering in the corner of the bedroom. She had told me through her tears that I had a blackout the night before and had beat her senseless.

When I told her my version of events the previous evening - waking up in my van with a dead girl, she had looked at me baffled and told me my brain must have been playing tricks on me while I had blacked out. We had never had a fight; she'd certainly never hurt anyone in her life let alone killed some poor innocent girl. No, what had happened, so she told me, was that we had been in the back garden hanging out the washing when suddenly I went nuts and attacked her. After I had finished on my rampage I had gone to bed without even a backward glance at my poor bleeding battered wife.

This was the first time I heard her speak of 'The Other One'.

I'd been devastated at the thought that I could hurt Linda like that. But at the same time, I was just so relieved to find out that the dead girl in the van had just been an awful vivid nightmare. This was the start of Linda demanding better medication for me from Dr Mandela.

Dr Mandela had every sympathy for poor Linda living with a psychopath who couldn't tell his dreams from reality, who became violent when his 'other' personality took over. She had stitched me up like a kipper. After all, who would ever believe my word over hers?

Up until this morning I had thought it must have been me that killed the dead girl, Linda must have been looking out for me, covering for me. I had thought poor pregnant Linda must be protected from me no matter what.

Not anymore.

My baby must be protected from her.

I had in my pocket the dictaphone I had borrowed from Philip. I was going to try and get a confession out of her. I think once she knew the game was up she'd stop pretending and start telling the truth. I needed her to confess to everything she had done so that she'd be locked up indefinitely. She was a lunatic, I knew that now. I would raise our child on my own.

I pulled into her dad's driveway, not really knowing what to expect. I didn't want her dad to hear what we were going to be talking about, after all, he had heart problems, I couldn't handle his death on my conscience. I'd rather he heard it all from a professional. If she was here, I would say I came to take her out for dinner or something, and then we'd go somewhere and talk.

I walked up the path of the large detached house. It was set back from the road, with tall trees shielding it from the traffic. I'd always found this house creepy at the best of times. It looked like something from a scary film, with its tall gables, large leaded windows, and abundance of ivy trying to choke everything it got a hold of. I pressed the brass bell button next to the door and waited.

Nothing.

I tried it again.

Nothing.

I banged hard on it with my fist. Turning around to view the front garden while I waited, I thought I saw the upstairs curtains of the house next-door twitch. I stared up at the window but couldn't see anyone, I wasn't sure if I imagined it. I huffed with frustration after knocking several more times. Why wasn't anyone answering? He was supposed to have someone looking after him at all times.

I fought my way around the shrubbery and tried looking through the large lounge window next to the front door, but the curtains were drawn tight shut. I didn't like this, something was wrong.

I started walking around the side of the house, trying to look through every window that I passed. Every single one had the curtains or blinds drawn. I tried the door that was set into the garden wall that divided the front garden from the back garden, locked. Shit. Never mind, I wouldn't be deterred that easily. I dragged the dustbin over to the wall and climbed on to it. It got me just high enough to be able to pull myself up over the wall, and jump down to the other side. Although the front garden of the house looked tidy, the back garden was a complete jungle. The acre or so of lawn looked more like a meadow than the manicured lawn I had seen every other time I had been here. I shook my head at the shock of it. I trod on a dandelion sticking up through the paving as I made my way to the back door. Once again, curtain drawn across the window, door locked.

Fuck it.

I ran at it and kicked it in. It took three attempts, but it got me in.

I put my hands over my face as I entered the kitchen to try and block out the stench. The air smelled really sour, like gone off milk, it was really unpleasant. After confirming that there was no one lying in wait for me in the kitchen, I pulled open the curtains to let some light in. Though I soon wished I hadn't. The table was laid with the remains of a meal, long ago devoured by the hundreds of maggots that lay writhing in the dishes.

"Ugh!" I backed away with horror. Holding my hand tighter over my nose to try and muffle the smell. Now I knew what it was, it seemed so much worse than before. I shuddered and made my way through the stinking kitchen to the dining room beyond.

I made my way around the large dining table to the window at the far side. I pulled back the drapes allowing the sunlight to flood in. Thankfully all this room contained was dust. The smell wasn't so bad in here, much fainter than it had been in the kitchen. I cautiously opened the door that led to the main hall. I could feel the hairs on the back of my neck starting to stand up on end. I crept across to the living room first, slowly twisting the handle. Peering around the door with one eye first, I found it to be empty. I didn't bother opening the curtains; I could see well enough that there was nothing of interest in there. That left me either going down the steps to the cellar (I don't think so.) Or going upstairs.

It was ridiculous me creeping around like this. I was here for Linda. I needed to talk to her. I needed to know if she was here or not. I took a deep, brave, breath and called up the stairs, "LINDA?"

I cringed at how loud I sounded in the death quiet of the house. Even the dust seemed to scatter from the shelves at the decibel disturbance. I strained my ears waiting for some semblance of life from above. Nothing.

"Shit." I said to no-one. "I'll have to go up there."

I started up the large Victorian staircase one squeaky step at a time. Any second I expected her to come flying down at me with a carving knife. My hand glanced off the light-switch as I made my way up to the next floor. "Light would be good." I flicked the switch.

"Ugh!" I fell back against the banister at the sight of the blood-stained wall paper I had been trailing my hand against. "Shit." I scraped my hand against my jeans with horror. My heart was thundering through my clothes, and I was starting to hyperventilate. I stood on the step for an age looking from the blood-stained wallpaper to the landing above me. Did I really want to go up there?

I had to. That monster was walking around with my child.

I took several deep breaths and started climbing higher. I'm gonna die here, I thought, as I rounded the landing. I couldn't see much in the darkness up here, so against my better judgement, I felt for the light-switch and flipped it.

Blood. Everywhere. The landing was about ten-feet-square, and circled all around it was a trail of bloody hand prints. It looked as though someone had put up a hell of a fight, and lost.

I stood staring for an age. My brain just couldn't take in what I was seeing. "I'm going to wake up in a minute." I whispered to myself. I looked down in horror to find that my hand was opening the first door without asking my permission. I pulled it back quickly, but it was too late, the door slid open slowly. This was Linda's dad's room, the master bedroom. The stench that came wafting out at me was horrific. I gagged and pulled my t-shirt up over my nose. I could see a shape lying in the bed, but it was too dark to see anything else. I shut my eyes and flipped the switch next to the door. I opened my eyes a tiny little bit and peered through my lashes at the bloated maggot-ridden corpse lying in the bed. "NO!"

I turned and vomited all over the floor. I stepped over the puke and out the door, pulling it firmly shut behind me. Linda's dad had been dead for days by the look of his corpse. As I stood with my back to the door panting my eyes fell on the blood trail on the wall. It seemed to stop at the door dead opposite me. I shook my head. "Please no more. I can't do this." My eyes were filling up and stinging. I stood staring at the door, paralysed with fear. I concentrated on just breathing, one little breath at a time, one after another, each one a little deeper than the last. The panic attack was subsiding a little. I stared at the door, and made my decision. Before I had chance to change my mind I turned the handle quickly and went in.

I shouldn't have.

The sight that I saw when I opened that room will haunt me till the day I die. Linda's cousin Josie, or rather what was left of her, was strewn around the room. In Pieces.

Her naked torso had been propped up into a sitting position on the large wicker peacock chair in the corner of the room. Her arms had been severed at the elbows, leaving a large chunk of exposed bone hanging from the bloody stumps. Her legs had been sawn off at the knees, badly. There were several failed cut marks were the saw had slipped. Her arms and legs were laid out on the blood-stained bed covers that covered the floor.

I turned around to see the saw propped up in the corner next to an axe.

I screamed in horror as I saw her head had been tied to the handle of the wardrobe door by its hair. The last moment of horror stamped forever on her young face.

It was all too much; I fell to the floor in a dead faint.

Chapter Thirty-One

I awoke in the dark to the sound of someone softly calling my name.

"Flynn? Wake up. Flynn, Flynn please don't be dead."

I tried to rub my eyes but found that I couldn't move. "Agh." I panicked and started fighting against my restraints.

"Flynn, can you hear me?"

"Yeah." I carried on fighting in a blind panic.

"It's me, it's Susan."

That made me sit up with a start. "Susan? You're alive?"

"Only just."

"Everyone thinks you're dead. You've been on the news all week."

"Your wife stabbed me and dragged me here."

"My god! Why?"

"Why? Because she's insane!"

"But why hurt you? She doesn't even know you?"

"She was screaming at me for having an affair with you. Apparently when we went for that coffee together, the waitress told her that we were getting VERY friendly and were holding hands."

"We weren't!"

"I know, I told her, but she won't have it." She started choking softly.

"I'm so sorry Susan. I had no idea what she was up to."

"I know, she told me."

I couldn't take it all in. "How did she get you here?"

"After we parted I went back to Bobby's house and managed to speak to him, he was okay, a bit out of it, but better than I expected him to be all things considered. Then I got a text from you, or rather from your phone, asking me to meet up. When I got there, Linda came towards me smiling saying that you had asked her to meet me, that she had something for me. She did alright; she stabbed me in the stomach with a carving knife. The next thing I knew, I was tied up here."

I started crying. "I'm so sorry, this is all my fault. How are you still alive?"

"I don't know how deep she stabbed me. It bled like hell for days. I kept drifting in and out of consciousness for a while, but I think it's stopped bleeding now. It stinks though, I can smell the wound, I think it's gone bad. Every time I thought I was going to die she'd feed me and give me water. She said she didn't want me to die too soon, she had too much planned for me." She started crying softly again.

"I'm so sorry. Don't cry. Where are we? Do you know?"

"We're in the cellar."

"Did she drag me down here? The last thing I remember was feeling faint upstairs."

"Yes. You've been here about ten minutes."

"So she's still up there?" I exclaimed.

"I can hear her walking about."

I listened carefully. She was right, I could hear faint footsteps. "Will she come back?" I asked.

"Oh yes. She told me when she's finished getting rid of the other bodies, I'm next. She said I'm only still alive because she's got a backlog. Is that true do you think?"

I nodded before I remembered that she couldn't see me in the dark. "Yes. There's at least another two upstairs."

"God." She started crying. "We're going to die down here."

"No, we aren't. I have someone calling the police to this address if he doesn't hear from me soon. We just need to stay alive for the next couple of hours until the police get here."

"Oh thank god!" she started sobbing with relief. "I just want to go home!"

"You will, I promise."

"My stomach hurts so bad."

"I know sweetheart but we'll get out of this soon, just hold on a little longer."

I froze as I heard the sound of the door being unlocked.

"Linda." I gasped with fear. She flicked the light on making me squint, illuminating the face I had so often thought of as 'the other one'.

She smiled at me. "So you found my dear cousin. Tut, tut, you shouldn't have gotten so nosey my dear. You do know that now I have no choice but to kill you don't you? I don't want to, but you've left me no choice."

I tried cajoling her; I needed to buy some time. "Linda, we can work this out. It doesn't have to end like this."

She smirked. "Oh yes? We can just go home and pretend it's all happy families, can we? To be honest I've been finding you hard work lately anyway. You're so needy. Do you have any idea how hard it is living with someone who is brain-damaged?"

She was out of her fucking mind!

"I'm sorry. I didn't mean to put on you so much, I promise I'll try harder. I'll put you first, you and our baby."

"Baby?" She laughed. "It isn't your baby. I've been sleeping with a fella' up the street for the last five years. That was one thing you had right." She laughed again shaking her head. "I have slept with half of our neighbours!"

"I don't believe it."

"Oh believe it baby. You don't know the half of my little adventures over the years."

"I know about the girl who you killed and buried in the cemetery."

She raised her eyebrows mockingly. "You mean the girl YOU buried in the cemetery."

"You made me believe it wasn't real, that it was a blackout."

"And you fell for it." She shook her head amused. "Sod it, I might as well tell you about the others too. It's not like either of you are going anywhere." She pulled up a wooden chair and sat in front of Susan and I - her own private audience. "You can't imagine how intoxicating it is. Having that much power, having your own private scapegoat, there ready to take the fall for you anytime you like. The bus incident changed me. It was like the world suddenly got brighter and darker at the same time. Anything suddenly seemed possible. You were getting all the attention all the time, and I just seemed to pale into insignificance in the eyes of everyone else. It left me time to think, to experience, to LIVE for the first time without guilt, conscience, or really giving a crap about consequences anymore, after all, why should I? I'd never get in trouble for any of it, you would." She pointed at me smiling with delight.

"The first time I killed was a mistake, a petulant temper tantrum, that was the girl in the van. But, with how easy it was to get rid of her and convince you that it never happened, it just opened up a new door of possibilities. My body count so far is eleven, until later when it'll go up to thirteen." She grinned menacingly.

My stomach dropped even further. "Who else have you killed?" I could still feel the Dictaphone in my back pocket, hopefully with the position I was sitting in the little record button would be depressed.

"Oh, it's hard to remember." She thought hard. "The first one you know, the next few you wouldn't know. Just people that pissed me off. Oh, Dr Mandela, I broke into her house and pushed that nosey bitch down the stairs. I think she was onto me. She kept trying to insist on me having another brain scan. No, she had to go. Actually, you should be thanking me Flynn, that bitch who grabbed your arm at work a few weeks back? The one that made you mad? She bit the dust. I drugged your coffee to knock you out and then strangled the bitch. I hid her body in the compost heap. You didn't know, but the coffee at work was my own personal blend of coffee and sedatives. That's why I only ever drank Tea. Did you not wonder why you always fell asleep whenever I sent you for a coffee to calm down?" She laughed at my shocked face. "Oh and then that little slut Elaine who gave you her number." She made a throat slitting gesture with her hand. "I got sloppy with that one though, I nearly got caught with the body and had to leg it quick." She started counting on her hands. "Let me see, who else have I killed that you might know?.....Oh you met cousin Josie upstairs? That little bitch was driving me mad. I came back and borrowed your van one night while you were asleep and went looking for her. I followed her from work and ran her down at the first opportunity. It took a bit of dragging her into the back 'cause she was still conscious, but her legs were broken so she couldn't get far. I kept her alive down here for quite a while." She smiled as though it was a nostalgic memory. "What really made me laugh though, was you fixing the van and cleaning all the blood off it. Did you really think that you'd done it?" She laughed like a maniac.

I shook my head. "Why did you cut her up?"

She looked up in surprise. "Well d'oh, easier to get rid of. Plus, it's fun! You'll find out!" She winked and laughed. "After Josie I took out that stupid male nurse, he got right up my nose snooping about where he had no business. He'll make good fertiliser though. Unfortunately my dad caught me chopping him up, so as much as I didn't relish the thought of it, I drugged him, and suffocated him."

"Jesus Christ! Where was I when all of this was going on?"

"Oh that's the funny part. You thought you wasn't epileptic? Oh you so are! When I wasn't able to drug you or knock you unconscious, all I'd have to do is shine a strobe light near you and off you'd go. Shaking and fitting in a pool of your own drool and piss. Then of course when it would pass, you'd be unconscious for hours. Plus, you wouldn't remember the events leading up to a fit. It gave me the perfect opportunity to go off and do whatever I liked, as long as I was cowering in a corner when you woke up everything would be fine. You'd feel so guilty for hurting me that you'd bend over backwards to look after me. It would've been quite sweet if it wasn't so pathetic."

My god!

She pointed her knife from me to Susan. "Now what I want to know, is how long you have been having an affair with this stuck-up bitch."

"There's nothing going on between us." I said earnestly.

"So why did my friend the waitress call me up and tell me that you had been in, holding hands and whispering together?"

"We didn't hold hands. I was helping Susan find her son Sid."

She leaped up pointing her knife at me. "Ah ha. Caught you out there then haven't I? She said her son's name was Bobby!"

Jesus Christ! This would take some explaining. Still, it would pass some time till the police got here.

"Bobby is Sid's real name."

"Oh how convenient!"

Susan chipped in. "He's telling the truth. Bobby is his real name, but his twin brother was called Sid. After Sid died, Bobby started referring to himself as Sid." She looked at me meekly. She knew how it sounded.

Linda ignored her and turned to me. "I read your phone. I'm not stupid."

"If you read my phone you should have seen that I was texting back and forth with someone called Sid."

She nodded. "Yeah, I did see those."

"Susan is Sid's mother. Sid tried to kill himself last week and went on the run when he thought he'd get put in an institution. I was helping Susan find him. That's all. I promise nothing was going on. I have never, ever, been unfaithful to you. I've never wanted to. You have always been the one."

She looked at me a little softer. "You really mean it? You two haven't been...."

"No." Susan and I said together, shaking our heads for emphasis.

"So this is all just a misunderstanding?"

"Yes." We both nodded.

Linda sighed deeply and then laughed a little, bemused even. "Oh well, shame it's too late now."

"It isn't too late Linda."

She looked at me doubtfully. "You must think I'm stupid. You know now all the things I've done."

"Yes but I don't care. I love you Linda. I always have."

She smiled. "I love you too." She sighed sadly. "I'm sorry for what I said before, about the baby I mean. It is yours, I haven't been unfaithful either, I just wanted you to hurt like I hurt."

"I'm sorry honey."

She came over and sat on my knee, head rested on my shoulders. She started to cry. "I thought you'd fallen out of love with me. I thought you loved her." She pointed petulantly at Susan.

"It's always been you Linda, you know that don't you?"

She nodded, tears starting to roll down her face.

"I'd love to cuddle you Hun, but I'm sort of tied up."

She looked sharply at me. "How do I know you won't run?"

I sighed. "Well it's trust me or kill me. The choice is yours Linda."

She looked from me to Susan. "I have to go think."

She gave me a kiss on the cheek, and climbed back up the stairs and closed the door behind her. At least this time she left the light on.

I turned my head to look at Susan. "We have to get the hell out of here, now!"

Chapter Thirty-Two

"She's insane Flynn."

"I know. We have to get the hell out of here. What are we tied up with?" I wriggled against the back of the chair trying to feel what was around each wrist.

"I think it's cable ties. At least yours are, I can see them from here. I don't know what mine are, I haven't felt anything in my hands for days. I think they're probably useless now." She started crying.

"Hey it's okay. Everything is going to be fine. Your hands have just gone numb that's all. Once the blood gets flowing again you'll be good as new."

"You think?" She sniffed.

"Absolutely." I lied.

I could feel the dictaphone still in my back pocket. I wriggled my arse until I worked the dictaphone up towards my tied hands. The device had a little metal hook on it that would allow it to be attached to a belt. By the feel of my cable tied cuffs, I had one tight around each wrist, and one more on the middle connecting the two wrist restraints. I reached up with the tips of my fingers and hooked the device onto the middle cuff.

Susan was peering over at me. "What are you doing?"

"I'm trying to weaken the cuffs and get us out of here."
Once the device was hooked securely onto the middle cuff,
I swung it with my fingertips so that it went up and over the
cuffs, creating a twist in the middle of the plastic tie. With a
bit of luck if I persevered I would weaken it enough to be
able to snap it. I grappled with my fingertips and swung the
dictaphone back up and over again several more times.
"Hopefully it should have weakened the middle cable tie
now." I told Susan, panting with sweat from the effort and
concentration it had taken. I pulled my hands apart behind
the chair with every ounce of strength that body and soul
could muster. I almost fell over as the cable tie snapped and
released my hands. "Oh thank god!" I cried. I wiped my
face with my hands with relief. I looked over at Susan who
couldn't speak for crying. "It's okay. Nearly there." I told
her.

I bent down to free my feet that had been cable tied to
the chair legs. This wouldn't be quite as easy. I looked
around me at the dimly lit cellar; across the far side of the
room was a work bench. Hopefully there would be
something I could use to free us both over there. I stood up
with my ankles still fastened to the chair legs and shuffled
across the floor a few inches at a time.

"Hurry!" Susan called.

Hurry? Was she fucking joking? I didn't comment, and
carried on my journey across the floor.

Inch by inch, I slid closer and closer to the work bench, fading from Susan's sight into the shadows. I strained my eyes to try and make out what the shapes were that were on the bench. Another few inches of my tired calves shuffling and I could almost reach. A little closer, I stretched my fingertips out to the object that I could just about see in the dim light. My fingers grazed it gently. It looked like pliers or something. I reached my fingertips out a little further, stroking the handle a little; I strained out a little bit more, sweat dripping down into my left eye blinding me with its salt. I blinked it away and got a hold of the handle of the object. I pulled it towards me, crying out with triumph. "Agh!" I dropped the pliers on the floor in horror at the human tooth that was still stuck in its teeth.

"What is it?" Susan called after me.

"Nothing. Everything is fine." With a thundering heart, I bent down and picked up the pliers, opening the handle so that the tooth dropped out before I had to look at it. The pliers would be no good at cutting through our cable ties, but I used them to reach the pair of wire cutters that had just been out of reach up on the shelf. Using the pliers, I pulled the wire cutters towards me. I held them tightly in my hand and bent down to free my ankles from the chair.

FREE!

The cable ties fell away along with the chair. I shot across the cellar to Susan, who seeing what I had in my hand gasped with relief. I clipped away the ties from her ankles first, wincing at the bloody ring marks around her flesh. "Sorry." I apologised as I pulled one cable tie out of her skin were the flesh had started growing back over it.

"It's okay. I can't feel anything."

Once her feet were free, I went behind her chair and started cutting away the ties that held her. She had been much more savagely tied then I'd been. No wonder she couldn't feel anything. I peeled the ties out of her flesh cringing at the blood that poured from the cuts ringing her wrists. I clipped the last tie away, freeing her completely. Her hands dropped to her sides uselessly.

"They're dead." She said robotically. "I can't move them. I can't feel them!"

"You have to give the blood chance to run back into them."
I picked her left hand up and rubbed it with my own hands to try and get the blood flowing. After a few minutes I turned my attention to the right hand.

"Pins and needles." She panted between sobs. She gave me a week smile.

"Pins and needles are good. It means they're waking up." I turned my attention to her ankles next. First the left one, massaging her freezing cold ankle and wiggling her bare foot back and forwards.

"Can you feel anything yet?"

"A little. I think I'm getting cramp in my feet." She wriggled.

I turned my attention to her right foot when I heard the cellar door clatter open. I turned in horror. "Linda!"

"Well this is very cosy I must say!"

I stood up and backed away from Susan. "Linda, Honey, she was in pain. I had to get those cable ties off her." I noticed the glint of metal behind Linda's back, for all her declarations of loving me, she had come prepared.

"How did you get free?"

"You didn't tie me up properly."

She frowned. "Is someone else here?" She looked around her, peering into the dark corners.

"Linda, put down the knife. Let's talk."

She ignored me and walked over to the far side of the cellar. While she wasn't looking, I bent down and picked up the wire cutters, sliding them up my sleeve to keep out of view.

"Someone's here. There must be. Who untied you?" She was sounding panicky. "Who's here?" She bellowed, sending her echo around the cellar.

"There's no one here. Linda? Let's go upstairs and talk. We were talking earlier weren't we? About putting things right?"

She looked at me with disbelief. "I just caught you fondling her feet? Now you want to talk? Are you insane?" She started coming towards me with her knife aimed towards my stomach.

"Linda she was in pain. I know you wouldn't want to hurt anyone, not really, not deep down. Linda you're ill, you need help. Let me help you." I started moving closer to her, getting ready to disarm her if I could.

She wavered a little, before finding her resolve and pulling the knife back up high in front of her.

"No. I don't want to hurt anyone. But I can't help it. IT JUST FEELS SO GOOD!" She lunged at me. I ducked out the way and spun around the back of her. I pulled the wire clippers out of my sleeve; I might need them after all.

She looked at them mockingly. "What are you gonna do with them? Nipple twist me?"

"I can cut your jugular."

"I die, the baby dies. But, at least you couldn't judge me anymore; you'd be a mass murderer too."

She had a point. I couldn't hurt my baby. She took advantage of my confused state of mind and lunged a second time. I side-stepped out of the way but left my foot sticking out. She tripped over it and went down like a deadweight straight onto the knife.

"Oh god no!" I cried and bent over to her. She was making a bubbled gurgling noise. "Linda." I whispered and gently turned her over. The knife was sticking out of the right-hand side of her chest, puncturing her lung. She looked up at me with wonderment. I could see the panic fading in and out of her eyes. "Hold on Linda. Everything's going to be alright. Just hold on. I'm gonna ring for an ambulance." She blinked hard at me, nodding her understanding.

I didn't have to ring for an ambulance, as I bounded up the cellar steps I came face to face with the police who had just come in through the broken back door. They had already called for an ambulance after seeing the blood everywhere.

"We need you to step aside Mr Locke." I was told by one policeman as I tried to go back down the cellar.

"But my wife's dying down there."

He looked at me with contempt. It wasn't my fault she was a killer.

"My friend's down there hurt too."

"I won't tell you again Mr Locke, get the hell out of the way!"

I was led by another policeman into the lounge, where I was questioned while waiting for the ambulances to arrive. I wasn't allowed to go in the ambulances with either of them. The police weren't finished with me. "But please." I said standing up and watching them take Linda out of the house on a stretcher. "Please will you tell the medics my wife is pregnant? She might be a lunatic but my baby isn't."

The irate police man replied. "We are well aware of that Mr Locke, now please, start again from the beginning."

I pulled the dictaphone out of my pocket and threw it at him. "Everything you want to know is on that!"

Chapter Thirty-Three

Once the police had finished with me I was allowed to follow on to the hospital. I rang Philip before I set off to thank him for sending the police, and to tell him what had happened. He decided to meet me at the hospital so that he could collect his car.

I was relieved just to get out of that house of death. I hadn't realised just how bad the smell was until I stepped out of the front door and breathed in the sweet air pollution outside.

As I was getting into Philip's car, an old lady came out of the house next-door and beckoned me over towards the fence to speak to me. "Oh god!" I moaned under my breath.

"Excuse me. Flynn?" She called over waving.

I approached the fence reluctantly. "Hi."

She looked at me earnestly; I didn't think she was after gossip after all. "I'm so glad you came."

Her voice sounded familiar. She saw my confusion and smiled at me sadly. "I'm sorry. It was me that called you on the phone. Your 'friend'."

The penny dropped. "Did you know about all this?" I gasped. "Linda?"

She shook her head. "No. At least not that she had killed anyone. I knew something was amiss. I went in one day a little while ago, and her father was in a terrible state. I got the impression that he wanted to tell me something, but Linda wouldn't leave us alone. Anyway, later on that night, Linda came around to my house and warned me that if I stuck my nose into her business again she'd kill me. I knew by the way she said it that she wasn't being dramatic. I was actually scared of her. I wanted to ring someone and warn them but what could I do? I knew the police wouldn't take a threat like that seriously, plus if they turned up asking questions she'd know it was me. That was why I called you."

I shook my head. "I'm sorry I didn't come sooner. I didn't know."

She smiled sadly. "One never knows what goes on behind closed doors."

I made tracks after that and got myself down to the hospital. Both Susan and Linda were shockingly on the same ward, I suppose with them both having stab wounds. I was torn between which woman to ask after first. My serial-killer pregnant wife, or my poor wounded friend.

I sat in the corridor while I thought about what to do.

A kindly nurse sat next to me and asked if there was anyone she could call for me.

"Sid." I said.

"Do you have a contact number for him?"

"No but he's on ward 40 under the name Bobby White."

"In this hospital?"

"Yes. Practically everyone I know is here somewhere."

"Okay." She said a little bemused. "I'll go see what I can do."

She left me with my thoughts then.

"Flintlock!" Sid called from the corridor. He was wearing a hospital gown and dragging a drip with him on stand. "Is it true? Is my mum alive?"

I nodded laughing with him at the relief on his face. "She's alive. But she's in a bad way. Linda kidnapped her and stabbed her. She'd had her tied up in a basement all week."

"Fuck me! I've just had a police woman in with me filling me in on some of the details. I can't take it in to be honest."

"Tell me about it. It isn't every day you find out your wife's a serial killer."

A doctor started walking past us. Sid shot up to question him. "Excuse me. Can I see my mum yet? Susan White?"

He looked Sid up and down, puzzled by the hospital nightdress by the look on his face. "She's in theatre at the moment. I'll know more in a couple of hours." He then walked off.

"Ignorant bastard!" Sid complained.

"I know. But at least she's alive Sid."

"And it wasn't even me that hurt her."

"I know!"

He sat down on the seat next to me. "So what's going on with Linda then? Is she gonna live?"

I shook my head. "I don't know. It's the baby that I'm bothered about not her."

"Oh shit yeah, sorry I forgot about the baby." He paused in thought. "Why'd she do it Flynn? Killing all those people?"

"Oh god you haven't heard the best bit yet have you?" It had been a long day. "It turns out I'm not brain-damaged at all. Linda was the one with brain-damage from the crash. Our notes got muddled up with us having the same name and almost the same date of birth."

"You're kidding me?"

"I'm not."

"But you're as mad as a fucking hatter?"

"Yep. But apparently that's 'cause I've been taking medication that I don't need. It's been messing with my head."

"So what happens now?"

"I've got to come off the tablets slowly. Because I've been on 'em so long I can't just stop taking them."

"Shit."

"As for what's going to happen with Linda? God knows."

"She's gonna get locked up in a nut house you know? If she lives."

"I know." I paused. "Do you think they'll let her keep the baby in there or will I get custody?"

"You'd get custody, especially now you're not a nutter."

I sat up sharply as a doctor came towards us. "Mr Locke?" He asked.

"Yes."

"We have just brought your wife out of surgery. We managed to repair the damage to her lung, and she's now in recovery. The operation went well, and we are pleased with the way she is responding."

"Can I see her?"

"I've been told by the police officer in charge that there is to be no visitors."

"Is the baby okay?"

"So far the baby is doing well."

Sid interrupted. "Do you know how my mum is? Susan White?"

"She's doing fine, she's out of theatre and in recovery. You can come and see her for a few minutes if you want?"

Epilogue

In the aftermath of Linda's trial, business at the garden centre went through the roof. At first I was horrified at the requests to see the compost heap where Linda had disposed of three bodies. But as Sid pointed out, they may come in to be nosey, but they all left after buying something. Takings were up through the roof thanks to all the free publicity we got from the media.

Sid came to work for me as my assistant manager, which was useful as I didn't have much time to be there with raising a baby.

Evie is the apple of my eye, a fat little bundle of cuteness that could shit for England. Even Sid gets grossed out. There's been many an evening where Sid and I play 'rock, paper, scissors' before one of us loses and has to change Evie's nappy.

Susan's been a godsend at helping out. I've never had a baby to look after before. I had no idea what I was doing. Once Linda had given birth, she kissed Evie goodbye and handed her to social services, who then handed her to me. (Without an instruction manual I might add.)

At first I was quite paranoid about Evie's parentage after Linda's revelation about having an affair with our neighbour. I had it out with him one day when I was having a particularly bad mood swing before I was properly weaned off the medication. After I had finished tent-pegging him to the lawn, (Literally) and approached him with my petrol lawn mower, he had sworn on pain of death that although he did have a regrettable affair with my wife, under no circumstances could he be Evie's father due to the vasectomy he had several years before. The large urine patch on his trousers forced me to believe he was sincere. Although once Sid had calmed me down somewhat and pointed out that it would have been much simpler to have had a paternity test taken, I did feel a little foolish.

Susan became Evie's honorary auntie and made life much easier for me by showing me how to be a parent. Although it was hard at first, Evie gave me something to live for again. She was my fresh start.

It took probably around three months before I could get back to 'normal' and come off all the tablets I had been prescribed for so long. I was moody and irrational, confused and arsey for a while before I started to get my equilibrium back. Now, with Sid, Susan, and Evie's help, I'm fine.

At first I tried to sell the garden centre, but due to it being the centre of a murder investigation I would have had to practically give it away. In the end, Sid made me see sense -which I'm glad he did. He came to help me out, he'd deal with the weirdo's who wanted to know all the gory details. He'd tell them he was the son of the only victim to survive, and if they would spend twenty-five quid on bedding plants he'd tell them all about it. For the first year it became like a twisted Jackanory. But by god did we make money.

Linda pleaded insanity, which nobody contested. The medical evidence and brain scans that her barrister produced were staggering. There was no getting away from the fact that she had been living with a massive brain injury that had been left untreated for nine years. She would spend the rest of her life locked up in an institution. But she didn't care, so she told the judge.

I on the other hand, sued the NHS for all I could! Mistaking me for being brain-damaged; treating me for brain-damage that I didn't have -which caused me to go quite crazy; and allowing my wife to roam the streets killing people, due to her undiagnosed brain-damage. Oh yes. They paid alright. The money is tied up for Evie when she's older. At least she'll be able to get a decent education if she wants.

I also have a new routine on a morning these days. Now, I get up, get dressed, look after my beautiful daughter, and go to work. It's good to have a routine isn't it?

But right now, Sid and I are getting the garden centre ready to open for tonight. It's Halloween and Sid is going to hide in compost heap number two, ready to scare the shit out of any of the ghost hunters that are camping here tonight.

They want to be scared? They came to the right place.

The End

Author's Note

The little pink pill is a story very close to my heart. My husband suffered from left-frontal-lobe syndrome after he was attacked and left for dead on the 2nd of September 2001 outside of a pub that we used to run. He died in the ambulance and had to be resuscitated during the 90-mph race to the hospital - where-upon admittance I was assured by the heartless doctors that he wouldn't live through the night and to 'prepare myself'. How the hell can anyone prepare for something like that?

I was twenty-one years old and about to be a widow.

Despite the pessimism of the hospital staff, he lived through the night, just. He developed a bleed on the brain that was causing too much pressure, so to monitor the pressure they screwed what looked like a metal antenna through his skull which was connected up to a monitor. I was told that if the figures on the monitor reached the number thirty they would have no choice but to cut the top of his skull off to relieve the pressure. I watched that monitor with my heart in my mouth for three days teetering on 29.9. Fortunately, the pressure started to come down after that, but then both of his lungs collapsed. Once again I was told to 'prepare myself', though fortunately my husband was a fighter and he pulled through and awoke from his coma a few days later. However, life is not always kind.

You can imagine my relief when his eyelids fluttered open and he looked up at me for the first time, though the relief was short lived when he said "Who are you?"

He'd forgotten me.

The year was 2001, my husband woke from his coma believing it to be 1983. He wanted to know where his wife Alison was. Alison had tragically died in a car accident in 1986, though for my husband this had not happened yet. He had to go through the horror of losing her all over again and getting used to his new wife and remembering my name, which became "Wife" most of the time when he couldn't remember it.

He was confused and bewildered at the world around him for a long time, believing that he was still normal, it was the rest of the world that had suddenly changed.

We had very little help or support from doctors, we never got counselling or respite care, and as soon as he could say the right date and give the name of the current prime minister (which he got wrong twice before he gave the right answer) - he was kicked out of hospital back to the pub that we ran. (Perfect place to recuperate, right?)

Like Flynn he was only given one brain scan, and sent home to "get on with it." His notes were often mixed up with other patients records too.

He had blackouts and mood swings like Flynn, often having no memory of the things he had done during a blackout. He'd have bouts of depression often culminating in suicide attempts, ongoing trouble with his memory, and some catastrophic mood swings. Plus a brief period where he thought I was trying to kill him. (I promise I wasn't.)

It took a while to get his medication right, though thanks to his little pink pill, he did much better.

We laughed together and took most things in our stride. It's true what they say you know, what doesn't kill you makes you stronger. He did know in the end that his perception didn't work properly anymore, so much of the time he relied on mine. (Poor sod, like he didn't have problems enough.)

Life was good for us, we learned to take the rough with the smooth and made sure to enjoy the smooth patches when they came along.

Sid was a real person that we met a few times at the hospital in the early days, though the real Sid was much scarier than I have portrayed in my book. The real one scared the life out of most of the hospital staff. We were regularly warned not to be taken in by his friendly manner as he was very dangerous.

The main reason I wrote the little pink pill was to vindicate my husband. He went through so much, worrying that he was the only sane person left in the world while everyone else was acting crazy, so I thought in my book, he really would be the only sane one. In my book, it really is everyone else.

Sadly I lost my husband last year when his skin cancer spread to his brain. Once again, I found myself by his bedside praying for a miracle, except this time it didn't come.

He really enjoyed the story of 'Pink Pill' and was proud that his extraordinary life had inspired it.

Thank you for taking the time to read my book and my author's note.

Kes xxx

Also by K. L. Smith

Flight of the Cuckoo

Cuckoo's Nest

Just a little Cuckoo – Coming soon

The Little Pink Pill

The P**e in the Jam Tart – Coming soon

20442917R00138

Printed in Great Britain
by Amazon